THE
IMPOSSIBLE
BOY

ALSO BY BEN BROOKS

Stories for Boys Who Dare to be Different

Stories for Kids Who Dare to be Different

Stories for Boys Who Dare to be Different 2

BEN BROOKS

THE IMPOSSIBLE BOY

Quercus

QUERCUS CHILDREN'S BOOKS

First published in Great Britain in 2019 by Quercus Children's Books

This paperback edition published in 2020

1 3 5 7 9 10 8 6 4 2

Text copyright © Ben Brooks, 2019

Illustrations copyright © George Ermos, 2019

The moral rights of the author and illustrator have been asserted.

A CIP catalogue record for this book is available from the British Library.

ISBN 978 1 786 54104 8

Typeset in Minion Pro

Printed and bound by Clays Ltd, Elcograf S.p.A.

The paper and board used in this book are made from wood
from responsible sources.

MIX
Paper from
responsible sources
FSC® C104740

Quercus Children's Books
An imprint of Hachette Children's Group
Part of Hodder and Stoughton
Carmelite House
50 Victoria Embankment
London EC4Y 0DZ

An Hachette UK Company
www.hachette.co.uk

www.hachettechildrens.co.uk

1

*A*s trees were being dragged into living rooms and tinsel was being wound around lampshades, Oleg and Emma sat at the back of their classroom whispering about how cold their ears were.

It was the Monday before Christmas.

A teacher was talking, and neither Oleg nor Emma was listening.

This teacher, however, was not the teacher that usually taught form 6Y about dead kings, exploding stars, and how to tell a million from a billion, because that teacher had fallen off a horse three days earlier. He wasn't supposed to have been on top of a horse at all and how he had managed to:

A. find a horse

and

B. get on it

were mysteries that remain unsolved. All we know for

sure is that he did fall off a conker-coloured horse and did break three semi-important bones in his left leg. Consequently, on that first day back, Mr Owen was drinking watery tea on a robotic hospital bed, and not taking the register or asking Scott Ballantine to kindly remove his finger from inside his belly button.

In his place, the students of 6Y had been gifted with that most mythical of creatures: a substitute teacher.

This substitute teacher was named Mr Clay. He wore sandals over bright socks, smelled faintly of milk, and seemed intent on foraging for snacks in his earholes.

'Good morning, class 6Y!' he gleefully called as he entered the room, leaning forward with one hand cupped around his ear.

No replies came. It was an achingly cold morning and no one was interested in being part of a pantomime. They were too busy trying to keep warm, stay awake, or stare longingly out at a playing field covered with a duvet of snow. Only a few sets of footprints broke the perfect sheet of white. It was snow that was waiting to be picked up and thrown.

'Let's try that again, shall we?' Mr Clay said, whipping the air with his hands. 'GOOD MORNING, CLASS 6Y!'

Still, no one replied.

Mr Clay's enthusiasm lasted an entire fifteen seconds. He

clicked on the flickering lights, kicked a mumbling old radiator, and wrote his own name in unreadable handwriting on the whiteboard.

Every member of the class was then issued with a piece of paper on which they were instructed to write a short essay introducing themselves and detailing what they'd done during the sub-zero weekend.

Form 6Y erupted into a loud mess of whispers, giggles, and pens scratching on paper.

Oleg and Emma decided to play a game that they'd been playing since the start of the year. It was a game that had landed them in trouble numerous times: inventing a new classmate. The reason for the game was simple: there were three musketeers, three little pigs, three French hens, but only two of them. There had been three of them until their third friend had been plucked out of their lives by her mother, who thought that Sarah Tuppet would have a nicer time growing up in a forest carpeted with bluebells. Both Oleg and Emma missed Sarah Tuppet. None of the other people in their class could take her place.

Ryan was too serious and too interested in the inner workings of trains.

Ora wanted to be friends with the teachers more than her classmates.

Tom talked so slowly that he never had time to reach the end of a story.

Scott Ballantine's main hobby was kicking things.

Callie never said anything that wasn't a lie.

And Elissa Goober was mean to anyone happier, sadder, or quieter than she was.

As a result, Oleg and Emma had been reduced to a two since the start of the school year, and they'd spent their free time imagining the kind of friend that could fill Sarah Tuppet's place. Of course, no one could really take her place, and the best thing that could happen would be for Sarah Tuppet's mum to decide she hated both bluebells and forests, but Oleg and Emma were starting to realise that wasn't going to happen.

'Quick,' said Emma. 'Write your essay then we can make someone up.'

'But ours should be good,' Oleg whispered. 'To make a good first impression.'

Emma waved away Oleg's concern. 'He probably won't read them anyway.'

'But what if he does?'

'Sir!' called Elissa Goober, thrusting her hand into the air. 'Oleg and Emma are talking!'

Mr Clay sighed and lifted his head. 'Do we have a

problem?'

'They were talking,' said Ora. 'I heard them too, Mr Clay.'

'And they were picking each other's noses,' blurted out Callie.

'We really weren't, sir,' said Emma. 'Callie always lies.'

'No, I don't.'

'Yes, you do.'

'Don't.'

'Do.'

'Please ...' said Tom Runkle, tremendously slowly. 'I ... am ... trying ... to ... work ...'

Scott Ballantine sent a kick into Tom Runkle's chair.

'Quiet!' bellowed Mr Clay, banging a fist on his desk. The eighteen members of class 6Y all flinched. 'You each have work to do and I'd appreciate if you got on with it, please. It may have escaped you, but I have my own pair of ears and am perfectly capable of hearing what is going on for myself.'

'I just thought you should know, sir,' said Elissa Goober.

'And I just think you should get on with your essay, Miss Goober.'

Elissa Goober scowled and returned to chewing on her pen.

Hurriedly, Oleg and Emma dashed their own essays off. Emma wrote about trying sushi for the first time, describing it as 'tasting like something you'd have to eat as a dare'.

Oleg wrote about finding a five-pound note on the floor, downing a litre of milk, and trying to catch a cricket in his bare hands.

Once they were done, they slipped another sheet of paper off the pile, and set about coming up with a third friend.

'What shall we call her?' Oleg whispered.

'It was a *her* last time,' said Emma. 'Let's do a *him*.'

'We could call him Tony.'

'No one's called Tony. What about Brian?'

Oleg wrinkled his nose. 'He's supposed to be our age.'

'Then Sebastian?'

'Right,' said Oleg, thinking that the name sounded unusual but not unbelievably so. 'Sebastian what?'

'Sebastian Winklevoss?'

Oleg shook his head. 'No one's going to believe that.'

'Sebastian Smith, then.'

'That doesn't sound right either.'

Emma thought and thought and finally came up with Sebastian Cole, which both of them agreed was perfect.

At the top of the blank page, Oleg wrote 'My Weekend' and the date, and, in handwriting that was trying its best not to look like his own, he added 'Sebastian Cole'.

Over what was left of the lesson, the two of them set about transcribing the weekend's adventures of a boy who didn't exist. It went like this:

My Weekend by Sebastian Cole

Hello, my name is Sebastian Cole, but you already know that. Well oh well I certainly did a lot of things this weekend, such as going on a boat to Australia and going on a plane to China. My family, as you may have guessed, are mind-blowingly rich, though we don't like to flaunt it. Our money comes from my great-grandfather, who invented . . .

Oleg and Emma turned to look at each other. His idea came first.

. . . the cheese grater in 1856. Before he invented the cheese grater, people had to chew cheese off the block like an apple or an ice-cream but thanks to him we can make it into little bits to go on top of pizzas or lasagnes or spaghetti bolognese.

Emma let out a howl of laughter.

'Is something funny?' Mr Clay snapped.

'No, sir,' said Oleg. 'I'm sorry. It won't happen again.'

Mr Clay tutted. 'No,' he said. 'It won't.'

Emma took over the writing.

But the best part of my weekend was when a snake attacked my mother. Don't worry, it didn't bite her. I put my hand into my bag, which is old but has everything I need inside, and I pulled out a baguette. If you don't know, a baguette is a type of bread that they use to fight each other with in France. Anyway, I whacked the snake with the baguette and it ran off and . . .

'Snakes don't run,' Oleg pointed out.

~~ran off and~~ crawled off and everyone was so happy that they bought me a small personal spaceship which aren't actually out yet but I have one. They said I was the bravest and that the snake was the most poisonous currently in existence. One single drop of its venom could kill one elephant and one tiger. Was I scared of the snake? Yes, but not as scared as I was of losing my mother, or my baguette for that matter.

By the end of first period, Emma had her entire hand in

her mouth trying to keep from laughing and Oleg was biting down so hard that his jaw was beginning to ache. He held himself together just long enough to finish the essay.

That was my weekend. And it was truly magical.

As they handed in their papers, Sebastian Cole's hidden between them, Emma noticed that Elissa Goober was eyeballing them. Whenever anyone was having more fun than her, Elissa Goober would eyeball them until they stopped having so much fun. She was that kind of person.

Oleg and Emma fled the classroom, hands pulled up into their sleeves for warmth.

*E*very day after school, Oleg and Emma would meet in their den. Sometimes they shared what was left of their lunches or invented games or imagined where their future lives would lead.

(Emma was intent on becoming either a dentist or a writer; Oleg dreamed of one day discovering a new species of insect and naming it after himself.)

The den was hidden in one corner of the school's playing field, behind a thick wall of hedges and under the branches of a vast oak tree that leaned over from next door's garden.

The den was all theirs. The only other person who knew it existed was the school groundskeeper.

Most days the groundskeeper would ride past on his sit-on lawnmower, or snowplough in the winter, wearing cowboy boots and a cowboy hat, with a leather sling holding the shears he used to shape hedges. The groundskeeper never spoke to either Oleg or Emma, though he'd seen them go into the greenery a thousand times.

The only problem with the den was that they had to speak in whispers while they were inside it. Gardens backed on to the school field and the inhabitants of those gardens had notoriously sensitive ears. They called school to complain about the noise almost every breaktime, every lunchtime, and every time a team trained on the grass after lessons. They hated school fetes and if you lost a ball over one of their fences, it was gone for ever.

In the dark, wooded space behind the hedges, Oleg and Emma sat on damp logs and blew on their freezing fingers as they discussed what Mr Clay would think when he read Sebastian's essay.

'What do you think he'll do?' Oleg asked.

'He can't do anything, can he? He doesn't know there's no Sebastian Cole.'

'What about the register?!'

'He didn't even do the register.'

'He must have forgotten. Doesn't mean he won't take it tomorrow.'

They both panicked, then realised that even if the register was taken, their substitute teacher had no way of knowing who had written the extra essay anyway.

'But I wouldn't mind keeping Sebastian around,' Oleg admitted. 'At least he did something exciting over the weekend.'

'I wish I could whack a snake with a baguette,' agreed Emma. 'This Christmas is going to be the worst one yet.'

'What about the one where you broke your leg and lost your front teeth and had to drink carrot soup through a straw?'

'Worse than that. Mum's going to be at work the whole time and Pip's sick so I'll have to stay in, the same as last weekend because stupid Oliver will be at his stupid girlfriend's.'

Pip and Oliver were Emma's brothers. One was six, one was sixteen, and neither of them saw enough of their mother.

'I thought you just didn't want to come out,' said Oleg, who had called his friend twenty-one times in two days and been told each time that she wasn't allowed to go sledging or snowball-fighting or snow angel-making in the field over the motorway.

'Of course I wanted to come out but Mum said I had to stay in and force Pip to take medicine.'

'That doesn't sound fun,' said Oleg.

'It didn't feel fun,' replied Emma. 'Are you doing real Christmas?'

Oleg shrugged. 'Probably not. Dad'll be asleep and I'll take four baths.'

'What about your nan?'

'I don't think she knows it's Christmas. When I asked if she knew what was coming up, she told me to have a happy Easter and gave me a pork chop.' He sighed. 'I tried cooking it in the microwave but it tasted like a massive rubber.'

Emma grimaced. 'Isn't it weird,' she said, 'that next year it'll be Christmas again but we'll be in another school?'

Oleg nodded. 'And we won't go in the art room or the music hut or see Elissa Goober or Tom Runkle ever again.'

'Why would you want to see Tom Runkle again?'

Oleg shrugged. 'I didn't mean Tom Runkle specifically. Just everyone.'

'I'll see Tom Runkle anyway. His mum knows my mum because they used to make burgers together at the bingo.'

'I don't care about Tom Runkle!'

They both sat silent in thought for a second. Oleg was trying not to think about the following Christmas, and how they might both be in different schools, and how he couldn't imagine anything worse.

'What if we made Sebastian official?' Emma said, seeing the look on her friend's face.

Oleg lifted his eyes from the snowy patch of ground he'd been staring at. 'How would we do that?'

She didn't hesitate. 'Tomorrow morning we get to the

playground early, say we need the toilet, and add him to the register ourselves. That way, we can write as much work from Sebastian Cole as we want.'

'We just put his name in?'

'Exactly.'

'What if we get caught?'

Emma shrugged. 'What can they do?'

Oleg thought that they could do very many things – shouting, detention-giving, claiming to be very disappointed – but he decided against listing them.

They spat into their hands and shook on it.

As Oleg and Emma left their den, the groundskeeper rumbled past on his clanking snowplough, leaving a deep track behind him in the snow. He tipped his hat to the children but said nothing. A long, thin blade of grass hung from the corner of his mouth.

At the school gates, Oleg and Emma said goodbye the same way they always said goodbye: by taking it in turns to gently double-tap the other person's forehead.

'See you tomorrow,' said Oleg, tap-tapping.

'See you tomorrow,' said Emma, tap-tapping back.

When he got home, Oleg found his father asleep on the sofa. His father was always either asleep or trying to fall asleep. A year earlier, he'd lost his job as a kitchen salesman and since then all he'd wanted to do was sleep. Oleg couldn't understand how his dad didn't get bored. He'd tried bringing him extra strong coffees and fizzy sweets and travel brochures for tropical islands, but nothing could convince his dad to get off the sofa.

Oleg guessed his dad's dreams had become more exciting than his real life. Oleg's grandma said Oleg's dad was just lazy.

This grandma, by the way, lived in the attic. She never came down. All day and all night, she sat up in the darkness, pecking at her big old typewriter.

Once, Oleg's grandma had been a great writer. She had captivated the children of Poland with wild stories of kids lost in jungles or deserts or on long voyages around fearsome icecaps and undiscovered archipelagos. She had told stories on TV, read in schools across the country, and been given a silver writers' award shaped like a giant pencil sharpener.

Then, after they'd moved across the North Sea to England, Grandma had found she could no longer write. She could start a story, and she did, hundreds and hundreds of them, but she could never work out how they ended. Kids were left trapped in forests, dragons remained un-slain, and whole kingdoms froze under her pen.

Oleg climbed the rickety ladder to the attic, opened the hatch, and slid a microwave pizza towards his grandma.

'Dinner, Grandma!' he called.

There was no reply.

There was never a reply any more, just the constant clicking of typewriter keys.

That night, Oleg fell asleep and dreamed that he really had spent his weekend on boats and planes and fought off a snake and been given a spaceship as a reward. It was a wonderful dream.

3

*E*mma woke up at five minutes past midnight. She was trembling. The cold had managed to make its way through her duvet as well as the three layers of moth-eaten wool she'd worn to bed. She shivered and felt the teeth rattle in her mouth.

The heating must have cut out. That happened sometimes, if mum forgot to add money to the meter. You'd be cooking pasta and the flames would flicker off, or reading on the sofa when the words were suddenly swallowed up by darkness.

Quietly, Emma tiptoed down the ladder of the bunk bed she shared with her younger brother and stood at the window, wearing her duvet like a cape.

Snow was falling gently on to the dim road.

Lampposts cast circles of orange light around themselves.

And out of the corner of her eye, Emma saw something move.

The hairs on the back of her neck rose.

Moving smoothly along as though they were hovering, a group of six snowmen came into view. At first, Emma thought they were people in costumes, until they came a little closer and she could see that each one was simply three boulders of snow, a stubby carrot nose, twig arms, and a pair of pebble eyes.

Emma dropped her duvet to the floor and pressed her face flat against the window.

She wasn't afraid.

Emma believed in a lot of things that couldn't be explained. She believed in ghosts and witches and tiny people who stole odd socks and lived under the floorboards. She wasn't sure yet about aliens. She thought the tooth fairy had probably once existed but was now in retirement after having finally collected enough teeth to build her ivory palace.

Moonlight picked out the shining eyes of the snowmen. They all seemed to be laughing with each other, weaving back and forth like close friends after a long night out.

Could they really be snowmen? Emma wondered. *There wasn't much else they could be. But where had they come from? And where were they going?*

Emma watched until the snowmen disappeared into the snowy night. She fought the wild urge to leave the house and chase after them, desperate to know where they were heading. She would have done it too, if her mum hadn't gone to work and left her with the task of watching over her little brother. Emma had promised not to leave him on his own.

Not wanting to get back into her cold bed, Emma threw her duvet over Pip and lay down next to him.

'Budge up,' she whispered.

Pip groaned in his sleep and rolled to one side.

'I'm asleep,' he whispered.

'I saw snowmen,' said Emma. 'They were laughing and walking up the road.'

'That's funny,' said Pip. 'Is this a dream?'

'I'm not sure,' answered Emma.

'My nose is cold in this dream.'

'My everything is cold in this dream.'

Emma put her mouth close to her brother's nose and breathed on it until some colour returned. They fell asleep tangled together as snow piled up on the pavements and laughing snowmen wandered through the empty streets.

4

The next morning, Oleg and Emma met at the monkey bars between the school and the field. As they tap-tapped each other's foreheads, Emma felt her stomach growl like a tiger waiting in tall grass. *Did he hear that?* she wondered. She hoped not. There hadn't been anything left for her breakfast after she'd cooked Pip the last egg. And the previous night's dinner had been delicious, but her portion was only about the size of a fingernail.

Her stomach grumbled again. To try and mask the sound, Emma started humming and tapping her foot against the icy ground as though an invisible band were playing beside them.

Oleg grinned. 'Here,' he said, handing her a slightly smooshed blueberry muffin from his coat pocket.

Emma peeled off the paper and pulled the muffin into two pieces, handing one to Oleg, who handed it straight back to her and promised he wasn't hungry.

'I'll only eat if you eat,' she said.

So he did.

As they ate, Emma thought about the snowmen from the night before. She had decided not to tell Oleg. She didn't think he'd believe her and she didn't feel like arguing. She wanted to keep her memory of the snowmen, quietly and fondly, like a photograph of someone that you missed very much.

Imbued with courage from the sugar, the two of them attempted to sneak into school.

They didn't get far. Mrs Havers stopped them two steps from the main door. Her rat, who had rather lazily been named Rattie, scampered up the slope of her neck and disappeared into the biology teacher's messy nest of orange hair.

Oleg took a scared step back. He still had a scar on one of his left knuckles where the creature had bitten him after he'd mistaken it for a strange kind of pencil case and tried to unzip it.

'Where exactly are you two going?' Mrs Havers wanted to know. 'It's not 8.30 yet. You know full well no students are permitted to enter the school building before then.'

'We need the toilet, miss,' answered Emma.

Mrs Havers looked between the two of them, sensing something suspicious in their smiling faces. 'Both of you need the toilet at the exact same time?'

'Yes, miss,' Emma answered sweetly. 'In biology you said we need to drink eight glasses of water every day or our brains will shrink, but I think we maybe drank too much and now we're fit to burst.'

To prove the point, both of them stuck out their bellies and patted them as though they were pregnant ladies.

Mrs Havers tapped her tangle of hair. 'What do you think, Rattie?' she whispered. 'Are they telling the truth?' In response, the rat tumbled out of her mane and caught hold of the biology teacher's earlobe. 'All right,' she said to the children. 'In you go.'

Mrs Havers stood aside to let them past. They *had* been told to drink a lot of water, and a common side effect of drinking a lot of water did tend to be a lot of visiting-the-toilet.

Oleg hurried away from the science teacher and her trusting rat.

Phase One was complete.

The two of them barrelled along the corridor towards the gym, only instead of turning left to the toilets, they headed right towards their classroom. Outside, Emma flattened her back to the wall. She pressed her hands together into a gun and pressed the gun against her nose. In a swift movement, she lunged into the room and swept the finger-gun from left to right.

'It's clear,' she said, relaxing. 'You keep watch at the door. I'll go in and add his name. If anyone comes, let me know.'

Oleg became panicked at the thought of being caught. 'How would I let you know?'

'I don't know, shout something.'

'Shout what?'

Emma rolled her eyes. She often thought her best friend was too thoughtful and that being so full of thoughts meant he worried too much. He had thoughts she'd never had. Once, when they found a lost kitten, he wouldn't let her give it milk in case it was allergic. 'How many cats are allergic to milk?' she'd asked.

'I don't know,' he'd said. 'Some of them must be.'

'When you see someone coming,' Emma told Oleg patiently, 'you shout: wow, this is terrible weather we're having! Then I'll know to hide. Got it?'

'I think so,' Oleg said, not entirely convinced.

'Repeat after me: wow, this is terrible weather we're having!'

'Wow,' Oleg repeated. 'This is terrible weather we're having!'

'Perfect.'

With a clearer plan in place, Oleg felt very slightly calmer. Phase Two began.

The coast was clear. Oleg stayed stationed at the door while Emma fell to the floor and crawled frantically into the classroom and under the desk. She tugged down the register and let it fall open on her lap. Most of the names were in alphabetical order but a couple had been added later, at the bottom, either because they'd been accidentally missed out or because they were unexpected additions to 6Y. Sebastian Cole would go unnoticed.

Unfortunately, the names were all written in red ink and Emma only had a pencil in her pocket. She yanked open one of the desk drawers and began searching for a red pen. It was full of strange and boring things: confiscated catapults, outdated mobile phones, dull coins, elastic bands, a single birthday sock. *Why keep any of this?* she thought. *And why isn't there a red pen?*

At the door, Oleg froze.

Someone was coming.

It was Mr Morecombe, the maths teacher who wore thick gold rings and breathed heavy salty breath. What was he doing in their classroom? Oleg wondered. The maths block was on the other side of the school. Oleg had never seen him here before. They only ever saw him on Tuesdays, Wednesdays, and Fridays. The dark days of maths and physics.

'Wow,' he shouted, rising on to his tiptoes. 'This is terrible weather we're having!'

'What are you talking about, Duchownik?' said Mr Morecombe, who was one of those old-fashioned teachers that preferred to address most people, even personal friends, by their surnames.

'The weather, sir,' replied Oleg, his heart pounding in his chest.

'What about it?'

'Just that it's terrible, sir, that's all.'

'Is something wrong with you, Duchownik?'

'I don't think so, sir.'

'Then why are you loitering about in corridors mumbling nonsense?'

Under the desk, Emma had located a red pen. She added Sebastian's name in handwriting as close to the teacher's as she could manage. Phase Three was complete. Now all she had to do was listen quietly to the conversation unfolding three feet away.

In the corridor, Oleg was struggling to come up with an answer. He worried far too much to be a good liar. To lie well, you can't be afraid of being caught, because the fear always gives you away. You have to believe in your lie so much that it no longer feels like a lie at all; that is the secret to lying.

So what reason could Oleg have for standing still outside an empty classroom?

'I've been sent to find you, sir,' he said uncertainly. 'And now I've done it.'

'Me?' asked Mr Morecombe. 'Why would you look for me here? This isn't my classroom. This isn't anywhere near my classroom.'

'Well you weren't in your room and you weren't in the art room and you weren't in the toilet and you weren't in—'

'Stop,' Mr Morecombe said, raising one hand. 'I get your point, Duchownik. What was it you were sent to find me for?'

'There's been an emergency,' Oleg lied. 'An important emergency.'

They stared at each other.

Oleg blinked. He couldn't think of anything more to say.

'Spit it out,' said Mr Morecombe. 'What's happened?'

'Like I said, sir, an emergency.'

'Duchownik!' shouted Mr Morecombe. 'I don't know if you've been hit in the head or are purposely attempting to aggravate me. What is going on?'

'Someone's let a goat into the school, sir. It's running about the geography block pooping on the maps. It's already chewed up shoes and carpets and—'

'Is this a wind-up? If this is a wind-up, I suggest you come clean now before I have the chance to get fully wound up. You wind me up fully, Duchownik, and I will explode, and you will be blown into pieces the size of chicken nuggets.'

'There's a goat, sir, honest. A real goat.'

'In the geography block?'

'That's where it was last seen, sir. Who knows where it might be now?'

Mr Morecombe threw his arms into the air and bounded away.

Great, Oleg thought. *He'll be back as soon as he realises there isn't a goat and I'll get an after-school detention and Dad will wake up for just long enough to confiscate my phone.* Why couldn't he think of anything more convincing than a goat? What kind of an excuse was that?

As Mr Morecombe disappeared around the corner, Emma emerged from behind the desk, register grasped in her hand.

She gave Oleg a thumbs up.

Mission complete.

'Why did you tell him there was a goat?' she asked, when they'd escaped to their den at the edge of the field.

'I don't know,' Oleg said. 'I panicked.'

'You shouldn't panic.'

'I don't choose to panic.'

It didn't matter. Sebastian Cole had officially joined form 6Y.

Abby Acheman
Scott Ballantine
Prianka Chopra
Oleg Duchownik
Elissa Goober
Callie Jones
Samuel Lugdogen
Emma Morley
Tom Runkle
Imran Samnani
Aaron Taylor
~~Sarah Tuppet~~
Ryan Weaver
Kirsty Wellandgone
Sampson Wiley-Corer

Rachel Kiley
Ora Looplooten
Sebastian Cole

5

The day started cold and got colder and then got even colder after that. One of the younger classes had been allowed to do lessons in the boiler room, where the clanking metal barrels radiated heat, but the rest of the school sat shaking in their classrooms, coats on and hands folded under their armpits.

The closer they got to Christmas, the less anyone wanted to be at school. They wanted to be curled up on comfy sofas, watching TV and obliterating crystals on their phones. They did not want to be learning about ancient empires or the correct place to put a comma.

Unwilling to do any actual work, 6Y had resorted to their usual diversionary tactic. It generally went like this: they simply had to keep asking their teacher questions that the teacher couldn't resist answering. If they kept a teacher talking, the teacher wouldn't be able to set them any work.

And they knew how to keep this one talking.

Mr Clay, they'd found out, was once an historian. If there's one thing an historian hates, it's hearing people spout incorrect historical facts. An historian can never resist the opportunity to set others straight.

First, Callie Jones raised her hand.

'Sir,' she said. 'Is it true that Romans wore socks?'

'Romans,' Mr Clay declared. 'Never. Wore. Socks. That's ridiculous. Where did you hear that?'

Callie Jones shrugged, grinned, and pointed at Aaron Taylor.

'Sir,' Abby Acheman asked, raising her hand. 'Where did Henry the Eighth lose his wives?'

'What do you mean "where", girl? He killed and divorced them. He didn't lose them. He got rid of them. You think he left them wandering around in the woods?'

Now it was Sampson Wiley-Corer's turn.

'Sir,' he said. 'Have there always been woods?'

Mr Clay looked confused. 'What do you mean, "have there always been woods?"' he said. 'What are you trying to ask?'

'Like, you know how there are woods now?'

'I'm aware that woods exist, yes.'

'Well what about before they existed?'

The bewildered teacher tipped his head to one side and scratched it. 'Before there were woods,' he said, 'there weren't any woods. Is that what you were asking?'

'Ignore him, sir,' said Emma, realising they were on the brink of being set a task. 'He's always silly. What we'd really like to know is how long would we live if we were born in medieval times?'

'Now that,' said Mr Clay, perking up, 'is an interesting question. It's a common misconception that people in the middle ages only lived until their thirties, but the truth of the matter is …'

And they could all relax in their seats as Mr Clay set about detailing how and why they all might die had they been born seven hundred years earlier.

Thankfully, they'd been born in an age of mobile phones, plastic water bottles, and biro pens, for these are the things that kept them occupied over the following hour. By the time Mr Clay was winding down his lecture it was almost time for morning break. Pencil cases began moving into rucksacks; feet began sliding back into shoes.

'Now,' Mr Clay said. 'I suppose you all think I'm dumber than a bag of rocks.'

Everyone paused. What was so dumb about a bag of rocks?

'I am fully aware that you were trying to waste both your time and mine. I shall not allow it, I'm afraid.'

There were groans from all four corners of the classroom.

'I have not given you that lesson for nothing. Following morning break, there will be a test. The test will cover everything I've been speaking about and more. You may spend the next half an hour revising medieval life, if you wish. As you seem to so enjoy asking me questions, a question shall be the reward. Whoever scores highest in this test will be permitted to ask me one question which I will answer as fully and as honestly as possible. You are dismissed.'

Everyone let out irritated sighs at the news. Not Oleg or Emma. If there was going to be a test, then Sebastian Cole was going to be taking it.

6

Two very peculiar things happened during morning break. The first took place as Oleg was stowing his pencil case in his rucksack, which hung on a hook in the corridor, below a shelf of wonky angels made from toilet-roll tubes and glitter.

Mr Clay was dawdling behind him, flicking through a book about fighter planes. He mumbled approvingly. 'Lovely wings,' he muttered to himself. 'Aerodynamically magnificent.'

Which was when Mr Morecombe rounded the corner. He was heading directly for Mr Clay, walking with his head up and his chest out. It looked as if they were about to collide.

And they did.

Mr Morecombe then walked briskly away without so much as a mumbled apology.

Oleg had never witnessed two adults behave like that.

Especially not in school. And the substitute teacher had only been there two days! What had happened between the two of them? He almost felt sorry for Mr Clay.

Almost.

He told Emma everything while they were cloistered in their den snacking on salt and vinegar crisps and drinking hot chocolate from a thermos flask.

'Maybe they already know each other,' she said.

'And they're enemies?'

'Could be. My Aunt Helen has an enemy. They call the police on each other all the time and make up crimes that the other one's committed. Like, sometimes my aunt says her neighbour has been stealing socks off washing lines and using them to make puppets, and once the neighbour said my aunt had been climbing into people's gardens and shaving their dogs.'

Oleg frowned. Did adults really behave like that? He hoped he never had to have a neighbour. He would live on an island, dry his clothes in a tumble-dryer, and be sure to buy the kind of dog that had no fur to begin with.

Emma tipped all the crumbs out of the crisp packet and on to her hand. Oleg ate a pinch, then she ate a pinch, then Oleg ate a pinch, and so on until the last crumbs of crisp were gone.

'He was near our classroom for no reason this morning,' Oleg said. 'And then he was there again for no reason just now. It's like he wanted to bump into Mr Clay.'

That was when the second peculiar thing made itself known.

A commotion was being caused out in the centre of the field. You could tell straight away that something had happened because there were no snowballs flying through the air.

Whenever there was snow, there were snowballs.

Unless something was going on.

Kids were huddled together, excitedly gabbling and pleading with Tom Runkle to give them more information. Tom Runkle, who was lapping up the attention, stood in the centre of the crowd with his arms outstretched.

'What happened?' Emma asked, bounding up.

'None of your business,' said Elissa Goober. 'Just go away.'

Tom Runkle ignored her.

'It's … Kirsty,' he said. 'She … saw … a … goat … in … school.'

Emma smiled to herself. First the snowmen, then a goat. Could they be connected somehow? Both seemed incredibly unlikely.

'What?' said Oleg, astonished that his lie had turned out to be the truth.

'She said … he … was … coming out of the toilet … and there was a goat just standing there … one leg up … whizzing on itself.'

Oleg and Emma exchanged looks. Maybe, Oleg thought, someone had overheard him lying to Mr Morecombe and was playing a joke? Maybe someone had overheard him and thought it sounded like such a good idea that they actually went out and did it? But where would you get a goat? At least, he thought, it might mean he would avoid getting told off for having told a lie.

'No way is there a goat,' someone said.

'Can you go crazy at eleven?' someone else asked.

'He's not crazy,' said Callie. 'I saw the goat too.'

'You never saw a goat,' said Prianka. 'I was with you the whole time. All you saw was what you found in your nose.'

'I saw it when you weren't looking.'

'You're such a liar, Callie Jones.'

When everyone returned to the classroom, numb with cold but thrilled at the prospect of seeing a goat, tests were placed in front of them. Emma stashed her first test under her chair then asked for another. She filled hers out in record time before getting to work on Sebastian Cole's, passing it back and forth with Oleg so they could take it in turns to make up answers.

Sebastian Cole, History Test

How many people died during the bubonic plague?

Alas, we can never ever know how many people died during the plague. There was no one to take the register, you see. Those poor, unregistered people.

What was the main cause of death during the middle ages?

Being born was the main cause of death during the middle ages. If you did not want to die, you had to try your best not to be born.

Why would a person have the job of graveyard warden!

Zombies were a common problem many years ago. Thankfully we do not have zombies today and so we do not need people to guard graveyards. In the past, your loved ones would pass away, only to rise back out of the ground and come banging on your peaceful door at night! You would be forced to shoo them away with a broom.

What was a knight?

I put it to you, sir, what wasn't a knight? A knight was not a king, we know that. But was a king a knight? No, mostly not. Could a baby be a knight? No, it would have to wait. What about a butcher? No, a butcher could not be a knight. A jester or a tall cousin could not be a knight. A poor person could not be a knight. A horse could not be a knight but a knight could be on a horse. A vicar could not be a knight but a knight could be friends with a vicar. That is what a knight was.

Once the time was up and all the papers had been collected, Mr Clay dismissed his new class. They all trooped through to the canteen for chewy beef, hard carrots, and a heated debate about how unfair their substitute teacher was being.

'That test was impossible,' said Abby Acheman. 'How were we supposed to count everyone who died?'

'I wish Mr Owen would come back,' lamented Scott Ballantine. 'Where did he even find a horse to fall off anyway?'

'I think Mr Clay's a fabulous teacher,' said Ora.

'You think all teachers are fabulous teachers,' said Scott Ballantine, rolling his eyes.

'Maybe they are,' said Ora. 'They know so much.'

Scott sniggered. 'They know so much about being idiots.'

'Don't … be … mean …' said Tom Runkle.

'Why not?' said Elissa Goober, leaning forward over the table until her face was an inch from his. 'Because you said so?'

Everyone froze. There were arguments, and then there were ARGUMENTS. Elissa Goober tended to go too far, being too mean and too loud, and almost all of them were too afraid to get in her way.

'Elissa,' said Emma, putting a hand on her classmate's shoulder and pulling her away from Tom Runkle. 'No one wants your face in their face.'

Elissa Goober shoved Emma's hand off her shoulder. The two girls squared up to each other and Emma tried to make herself look far braver than she felt. She bit down on her teeth and scrunched her toes up inside her shoes.

For a second, it seemed as though there might be a fight.

But no.

Elissa raised one eyebrow and tilted her head to one side. 'Your trousers have a hole in them,' she told Emma. 'I can see your pants. Don't you think it's time you bought new rags?'

Emma felt her cheeks light up red.

Elissa Goober scooped her milkshake off the table and stalked out of the cafeteria.

✳

After school, in the den, Oleg and Emma tried to make sense of their day.

'I'm sorry that Elissa Goober exists,' said Oleg.

'It doesn't matter,' said Emma, shrugging it off. 'But what about the goat? How do you explain that?'

'I can't,' said Oleg. 'But we still don't really know there actually was a goat.'

'Everyone says there was.'

Oleg folded his arms. 'I think one person probably pretended to have seen it and then everyone else wanted to have seen it too. Like that time Prianka said she saw the prime minister in the IT room and everyone else said they'd seen him too and it turned out to be Samuel's dad bringing him his packed lunch because he left it at home.'

Emma laughed.

'But it still doesn't make any sense,' Oleg continued. 'And I'm sure no one overheard me talking to Mr Morecombe.'

Emma shrugged. 'My mum says that people see what they want to see.'

'Why would people want to see goats?' Oleg asked.

Emma wondered again about whether she ought to tell him about the snowmen. She decided not to. If he didn't believe there had been a goat, she thought, it was unlikely he'd believe there'd been a gang of snowmen wandering past her window.

They emerged from their den to the sound of a hyperactive choir rehearsing 'In the Bleak Midwinter'. The painful tangle of voices soared through the roof of the music room and floated up into the dim grey sky.

'See you tomorrow,' said Oleg, tap-tapping Emma's forehead.

'See you tomorrow,' said Emma, tap-tapping back.

Emma left Oleg alone with his thoughts in the shade of their den. As she stepped out of the bushes, the caretaker in the cowboy hat drove past on his snowplough, loudly whistling an unfamiliar tune. He nodded when he saw Emma. She waved back.

*E*mma's family used to be poor and then they became very poor. She only realised this when she visited other people's houses, and found that the heating stayed on, tea bags didn't have to be reused, and their mums never said they'd 'eat something later' when everyone else sat down for dinner.

('Everyone else' for her meant Emma, her two brothers, and her Grandpa Lewis, who couldn't live alone any more and mostly stayed locked in his bedroom listening to the radio and eating slices of ham straight from the packet.)

The way they'd moved from poor to very poor was her mum taking out a loan and then another loan to pay off that loan and then another loan to pay off that loan and by now you're probably starting to understand what had happened.

The problem with the loans was that the companies that gave them charged interest, which just meant that the less money you could pay them, the more money they'd ask for, until you couldn't pay any at all, and grisly men would barge into your house and take your TV.

Years ago, Emma's mum had been studying for a degree in business, as well as working in a bookshop so big you could get lost in it. Once the loans started piling on top of each other, she had to stop studying and switch to working two jobs at once.

Emma didn't like to talk about it.

She'd never told Oleg. She wasn't sure why. She knew he wouldn't be hurtful about it, she just didn't feel like bringing it up.

Besides, the grisly men never took books. They were only interested in electrical things and gold things and very old things.

As Emma pushed open the front door, she was pleasantly surprised to hear her mum's laughter bouncing through the house. Her mum was hardly ever home. In fact, her mum was at the house so rarely that Emma had begun to wonder if it still counted as her home, or if it would be more accurate to say that she lived at the night café, occasionally visiting the building where her children slept.

'And where have you been?' her mum asked, smiling tiredly as Emma flopped down next to her on the sofa.

'Just in our den.'

'Oh really. And where's this den?'

'The field at school.'

Her older brother, Oliver, laughed.

'Surprised that old cowboy doesn't ferret you out,' he said. 'Still zipping around on his lawnmower?'

'I saw him today,' said Emma. 'He's still there. On a snowplough at the moment.'

'Wait a second!' cried her mother. 'That man was in the school when I was a tiny girl! The cowboy caretaker we used to call him. He was always drifting about with his big hat and his boots, nodding mysteriously at people.'

'We called him the rodeo gardener,' said Oliver.

'It can't be the same person, surely? He was old when I was young.'

'And now you're so old,' Oliver said, 'that he'd have to be double old.'

Mum flicked her eldest son. 'Who are you calling old?'

'You, darling mother,' Oliver cooed back.

'I'll give you darling mother in a minute.'

'Who wants tea?' Pip called from the kitchen.

'Two sugars,' shouted Mum.

'Three sugars,' shouted Emma.

'Four sugars,' shouted Oliver.

Dinner consisted of very tiny plates of minty lamb, glazed carrots, and a gravy so thick you could have spread it on toast. Cooking was Oliver's passion. But they often couldn't afford the necessary ingredients so either had to grow them or forage for them in the spindly woods that ringed the town.

One day he hoped to open a restaurant. The restaurant, Oliver claimed, would be on a mountain or at the bottom of a lake, and it would serve massive dishes that no one had ever heard of and have a waiting list ten years long.

Emma ate slowly, lost in thought.

How could the same caretaker have been there when her mum was young? she wondered. And how could a goat have appeared right after Oleg lied about there being a goat? Was the goat really connected to the snowmen? Or was it a coincidence that two impossible things had happened in two days?

Thinking about it wasn't getting her anywhere. She would have to stay awake and see if the snowmen returned.

After dinner, Emma took one of her favourite books into the cupboard under the stairs. It was the cosiest place in the entire house because it was where her mother stored all of the odd socks. Once a year, they'd spend a whole day trying to match them into pairs. The rest of the time, Emma just used them as pillows.

She made herself comfortable and opened her book. Before long, she'd tipped forward, and was snoring face-down on page fifty-five of *Emil and the Detectives*.

Emma didn't wake up in the night, which meant that she did not see the entire street packed with snowmen, raising their twig arms to the sky.

8

By the time Oleg got home, it was already dark. He'd been wandering around in circles.

Best of all he liked when the lampposts started to flicker on. It made him feel as though the world was being lit up just for him.

As usual, Oleg's dad was asleep on the sofa.

Oleg took the old, sweaty blanket off his dad and replaced it with a clean one. He put the old one in the dishwasher along with his own school shirt, his own socks, and two grimy tea towels.

On some level, Oleg knew that the dishwasher was for dishes and the washing machine was for clothes. But the dishwasher was quicker and less complicated and didn't they both do the same thing really?

He ate a microwave lasagne.

And eight squares of white chocolate.

And half a sour tangerine.

Then he cooked a frozen pizza for Grandma and carried it up the ladder into the attic.

'Dinner, Grandma,' he called into the darkness, same as always.

And, same as always, he expected there to be no reply.

Except this time there was.

'Oleg?' called Grandma. 'Is that you?'

She spoke to him in Polish. Sometimes, Oleg would lose the words he needed to answer her and feel ashamed. Almost all his dreams were in English by now. On birthdays, he'd be forced to speak to relatives back in Łeba on the phone. 'What's he saying?' they'd ask each other. 'I can't understand what the boy's trying to say.'

'I'm here, Nan,' said Oleg. 'Is everything okay?'

'What was that thud? I could have sworn I heard a thud.'

'It was Dad, he fell off the sofa.'

Grandma pulled a cord that turned on a light bulb, illuminating the entire attic.

Suddenly Oleg could see that the sloping ceiling was completely filled with Post-it notes covered in tiny, dense writing. There were pictures too: sketches of girls and boys and endless forests and monsters packed with razor-sharp teeth. Notepads were piled high and teetering stacks of paper were arranged in walls along either side of the room.

'He's a lazybones, that one,' said Grandma. 'A lazybones and a good-for-nothing.'

'He's good for lots of things,' protested Oleg. 'He's good for fishing.'

'Do you see any places to fish on this damp little island? Besides, the fishermen here catch the fish then throw them right back. That's the rules here, would you believe it? Now tell me, what's the point in that?'

Oleg couldn't see the point.

'Your dad has given up, and you're not allowed to give up, especially not when you have a child.'

'I'm okay,' said Oleg.

'Don't be ridiculous,' said Grandma. 'No one's okay. Now,' she said, patting the seat next to her, 'come and sit up here.' Oleg did as he was told. 'How are you getting on at school?'

Oleg wondered whether to try and tell her about Christmas. He decided not to. She'd only worry, forget, and remember six months later, when he'd be presented with a heavy scarf in the heart of summer.

'It's fine,' he said.

'"Fine," he says. He says he's getting on fine.'

'I am!'

'Let's hope so. You'll have to send us back home, one day, first class.'

'First class, Nan. I promise.'

Grandma sighed. Oleg imagined her picturing the sea at home, stretching out towards a sky the colour of grapefruit. 'You're a good boy,' she said.

'How's writing?' asked Oleg.

'Same as ever,' Grandma said. 'I start, I send these characters off into the world, then I don't know how to get them home.'

'Why don't you do something else for a while? You could come downstairs and we could play Snap with Dad.'

'That would mean surrender,' Grandma said. 'And I shall never surrender! It is of vital importance that things continue to be made up. As many things as possible, remember that. Everything that exists today started life as an idea in someone's head. Even you.'

'Oh,' said Oleg, not sure how he felt about that.

Grandma went on. 'It is crucial,' she said, 'that you train the imagination like any other muscle. If you don't work it, it will shrink and turn grey and eventually drop off completely like a lizard's tail. You'll be standing in a supermarket one day and realise you can't imagine a day any different to the one you're stuck in.'

'Okay,' said Oleg.

'Always see more than what is there,' Grandma told him. 'If they show you a pauper, be sure to see a king.'

'I'll try,' Oleg said, despite not being quite sure what a pauper was.

'Good, now shouldn't you be getting to bed?'

'It's quarter past eight.'

'What time's bedtime?'

'I don't really have one.'

Grandma clucked. 'Well,' she said. 'You ought to pick one and stick to it.'

That night, Oleg fell asleep at three minutes past midnight. The radio next to his bed was tuned to the shipping forecast: a slow, soft voice explaining how the weather was changing over distant patches of sea. Oleg wasn't awake to hear it, but the newsreader reported strange happenings in the North Sea. For half an hour, the water had become perfectly still, and great stalks of green lightning had jumped from the clouds. Rather than crackle and disappear, the lightning had spread like a web over the water.

That night fishermen stood on the decks of their boats, mouths open in surprise as the ocean glittered below their feet.

9

I n the white light of morning, Oleg prodded his sleeping dad. It was something he did from time to time, to check that he was still alive.

'What?' roared Dad, hurling a pillow across the room.

'Nothing,' whispered Oleg, backing away and gathering up his rucksack.

He still held out hope that one day his dad would blink awake and offer to walk him to school. Or he might even suggest that they skip school altogether and spend the day fishing at the carp pond or eating cereal out of the packet, like they used to. Oleg missed his old dad and was afraid of the new dad that had taken his place. The new dad was a snoring monster. The scariest thing about the monster was how much it looked like his old dad, even if it didn't smell right or make pelmeni or ever want to watch quiz shows and shout when someone gave a silly answer.

'Oleg!' his dad called out. 'I'm sorry.'

But Oleg had already left.

Nine months and three days earlier, a dog had bowled through the garden fence and bitten Oleg squarely on the leg. The dog had refused to let go. Oleg had screamed for help but his father had been sleeping. It was up to the neighbour to crawl through the fence and wrench the beast off him.

The dog left behind a scar shaped like a crescent moon.

When Dad realised what had happened to Oleg, he started sleeping even more. He refused to even look at the scar.

Oleg became afraid of any animal larger than a human hand.

✳

At the school gates, Oleg met Emma and they tap-tapped each other on the forehead. They weaved around the few kids standing on the field and made their way towards the den.

They waited to check no one was watching before going in.

But something was wrong.

There was a sound coming from inside the den.

It didn't sound human and it didn't sound animal either.

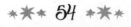

It sounded like a panicked computer, trying its best to work out a difficult sum.

Someone's found it, they both thought.

Someone's found our den and now we'll have nowhere to go.

'You go first,' said Oleg.

Emma rolled her eyes.

Oleg and Emma entered their den to find a cardboard spaceship standing exactly where they usually sat. The spaceship was blooping and bleeping and puffs of steam were rolling out of its hand-drawn panels.

Slowly, the front door opened.

Smoke billowed forth.

And out stepped a boy, dressed in a long coat with an even longer scarf wound around his neck. On his feet, he wore old boots spattered with mud, and in his left hand he held a satchel that looked as though it had once belonged to a painter. His socks were odd, his hair stood on end, and his cheeks were smeared with dirt. He smiled.

'My name's Sebastian Cole,' the boy said. 'But you already know that.'

Oleg and Emma stared at each other in disbelief.

The boy grinned innocently.

'What?' Oleg said.

'Who?' Emma asked, thinking she couldn't have heard correctly the first time.

'My name's Sebastian Cole,' the boy repeated. 'But you—'

Emma cut him off. 'All right, all right,' she said. 'You don't have to say the whole thing again. Just tell us who you really are.'

The boy looked wounded. His bottom lip quivered as though he was about to cry.

'I'm sorry,' Emma said, feeling bad. 'Say it if you want.'

The boy lit up. 'I'm Sebastian Cole,' he said. 'But you already know that!'

'Sebastian,' said Oleg, smiling his most polite smile. 'Could you give us a second?'

The boy nodded. 'I need to get to work on my ship anyway,' he said. 'She's busted a critical gasket and the ooberator's hotter than two lobsters in a sock. Blasted thing! I was passing through a spot of turbulence when this great goose came honking out of a cloud and smacked against my windshield. I expect the goose was blind, or at least blindfolded, but it gave me rather a shock, as you can imagine.'

Oleg pulled Emma out of the hedge and on to the school field. Around them, other kids were milling about and playing in the snow like it was a perfectly normal day. Oleg was as white as a glass of milk.

'How can Sebastian Cole be real?' he said.

'And in our den?' asked Emma.

'And it sounds like he's learned the lines from the essay.'

'Or he *is* the lines from the essay,' suggested Emma, more excited than she was shocked.

Oleg's head hurt. 'This makes no sense. What are we supposed to do?'

'There's only one thing we can do. Take him to class. He's already on the register, no one can prove he's not supposed to be there.'

'And then what? He's weird. People are going to ask who he is.'

'He's not that weird.'

'He just said "hotter than two lobsters in a sock".'

'That does sound kind of hot.'

Oleg rolled his eyes. 'You're just defending him because you made him up.'

'We both made him up and if he is *that* Sebastian Cole then we have a responsibility to look after him.'

Oleg sighed. 'Then we ought to get him, we're going to be late.'

They both stepped back into the den.

'Hi, Sebastian,' said Emma, cautiously. 'Form's about to start so we should probably all get going.'

'Brilliant news,' said Sebastian. 'The ooberator's turned itself inside out completely. I'm sure as stone not getting anywhere in this thing. Wretched machine! Actually, that's unfair. I'm rather fond of it. It was a present from my father, you know. He can juggle, which is a way of keeping all of your apples in the air at once.' Sebastian Cole cleared his throat. He seemed capable of talking for entire paragraphs without taking a breath. 'So,' he said. 'What are your names?'

'I'm Oleg,' said Oleg.

'I'm Emma,' said Emma.

And they all shook hands.

'Sebastian?' said Emma.

'Yes?'

'The other kids in form tend to be a little cold towards new people. So it might be best if you don't say very much.'

'My lips are zipped!' bellowed Sebastian Cole. 'You will hear not a peep from me!'

Oleg raised his eyebrows.

Emma shrugged.

As predicted, every pair of eyes in 6Y turned to face Sebastian Cole as he entered the form room. It was like a class full of owls spotting a worm. People began muttering amongst themselves. Was he an exchange student? Someone's brother? A new classmate?

He certainly didn't dress like someone from their school, or even really from their time period. He looked like a character from a book where pickpockets slunk through grimy alleyways. And he walked strangely too, as though everywhere he went, he was avoiding pieces of broken glass.

Sebastian took a seat between Oleg and Emma and placed his old satchel on the table in front of him.

When everyone was settled, Mr Clay swept into the room.

He searched the desk for the register but couldn't find it.

'Stupid thing's missing again,' he muttered. 'We'll just have to skip it for today.'

Someone coughed.

Mr Clay looked up.

'Sir,' Elissa Goober said. 'Who's that?'

'Who's who?' asked Mr Clay.

'That boy there.'

She aimed her spindly finger at Sebastian.

'It's rude to point,' said Mr Clay. 'You are not a monkey and neither is that young man. If you've forgotten someone's name, feel free to ask them yourself. Manners cost nothing, Miss Goober.'

'I'm Sebastian Cole,' Sebastian Cole told the class. 'But you already know that.'

Oleg buried his face in his hands.

'Ah,' Mr Clay said. 'Sebastian. What a thoroughly entertaining essay you wrote about your weekend, even if I can't say I believed every single word of it. The cheese grater, the snake, I wasn't sure what to believe.'

Elissa Goober looked bewildered. Oleg could guess why: everyone was certain this boy hadn't been in their form before. If he'd been there on the first day, surely they'd have remembered?

'Thank you kindly,' said Sebastian Cole. 'Though I can assure you that every single word of it was the truth, the whole truth, and nothing but the truth. Once I told a lie and ended up losing my smallest fingernail. What a night! I promised my mother then that I would never lie again.'

Everyone was staring.

Oleg *shhh*ed him.

Sebastian Cole didn't take the hint.

'I would not tell a lie, sir, even if you paid me one hundred thousand pounds.'

Mr Clay looked confused. 'That's good to know, Sebastian,' he said. 'I'll bear that in mind.'

The rest of the lesson was spent learning about long-dead armies squabbling over countries that no longer existed.

Once they'd been set a task to complete IN SILENCE, Oleg wrote a note and slipped it to Emma. It said:

We can't take him back to the den. Everyone else will be following. Somewhere else?

Emma passed back a note that read:

Let's take him up to the roof. We'll have to get out before everyone else and FAST.

When the bell rang, they grabbed Sebastian Cole by the hand and ran out of the classroom before anyone could follow.

10

The route to the roof was a secret that Emma and Oleg had discovered during their second year at the school. To get there, you had to go into the music room, climb on top of the grand piano, push up a ceiling tile, and help pull each other through. From there, you'd see a chink of light and crawl towards it, before emerging on the roof of the school.

They could see the whole of their town from up on the school roof, frozen under a layer of snow.

There was the grey supermarket, the crooked church, the greasy chip shop, the playground decorated with bright graffiti, the community centre where Oleg used to do gymnastics, and the park where Emma once met a woman who could talk to pigeons.

They lay on their backs, watching their breath turn to clouds as it drifted into the clear blue sky. Up on the roof, there was nothing to keep the wind away, and they were all soon shivering.

'It's rather chilly,' said Sebastian Cole. 'And I'd rather be rather warm. As well as unhungry. Is that the word, unhungry? Or full? Or fit-to-burst? Once I ate nineteen chicken nuggets in one go, without mayo, which is short for mayonnaise. What's the most you've ever eaten?'

'I don't know,' said Oleg, trying his best to keep up.

'Three Yorkshire puddings,' said Emma.

'I see,' said Sebastian Cole. 'And a Yorkshire pudding is a kind of cup made out of pancakes?'

'Almost,' said Emma.

As if the solution lay within, he began rooting around inside his satchel. A few seconds later he produced three large cones of ice-cream and passed them out to Oleg and Emma. Both stared uncertainly down at the freezing sweets in their hands. Neither of them felt like eating ice-cream in the biting cold but neither of them wanted to be rude either.

Oleg took a bite.

And then another.

Rather than turn his mouth numb and give him brain-freeze, the ice-cream warmed him like a toasty fire. He felt the blood moving through his fingers and the feeling return to his ears. Greedily, he wolfed down more.

'But how?' muttered Oleg between bites.

'Who cares?' said Emma.

They ate their ice-creams, then Sebastian Cole produced more.

Four ice-creams later, the three of them lay back, satisfied. Their mouths were sticky and their hands were stickier. Emma let out a burp and giggled.

'Everyone in your class was very interested in me,' said Sebastian. 'I wondered if there was some kind of disgusting creature perched on my head.' He passed both hands over his head as if to check. 'Once I found a lizard up there,' he said. 'It was trying to unwrap a Kit Kat.'

'You don't have anything on your head,' Emma reassured him.

'You're just unexpected,' said Oleg. 'We didn't expect you. People don't usually appear, especially not when we want them to. Do you know how you got here?'

'I'm not entirely sure. First, I was playing in my rocket, which my parents gave me as a reward for saving my mum from a snake with a baguette while—'

'We know,' said Oleg.

'And when I stepped out of it, I was in some kind of very small forest.'

'Our den,' said Emma.

'And you two were standing there, looking rather confused.'

'He knows as much as we do,' Oleg sighed.

'How much do you know?' asked Sebastian Cole.

'Not a lot,' explained Emma. 'Only that one day we were writing about you, and the next day you'd appeared.'

'You were writing about me!' He slapped his thigh as though it all suddenly made sense. 'Why were you writing about me?'

'We used to have this other friend,' said Emma.

'Then she went away,' said Oleg. 'And after that we tried inventing new friends because everyone else in our class is too loud or quiet or mean or boring.'

'What happened to your other friend?'

A faint shadow of sadness passed over Emma's face. 'Her mum made her move,' she said. 'She thought it would be better to grow up in the countryside because the city is too dirty and dangerous.'

Both of them looked downcast at the mention of Sarah Tuppet. The arrival of Sebastian meant they'd briefly managed to forget that they were missing their third friend.

Sebastian nodded seriously. 'A city is a place where people sleep piled on top of each other,' he said.

'Sort of,' said Oleg. 'They sleep on beds, in houses.'

'Yes,' said Sebastian. 'Just as I thought. On beds.'

That was when the bell chimed. On the playground, kids jostled each other as they raced towards the school building, leaving behind a scattering of breadcrumbs and shiny foil.

'What do we do?' said Oleg, suddenly panicked at the prospect of having to look after an impossible boy.

'What do you mean, what do we do? Sebastian's here now, we ought to take him to lessons.'

Oleg threw up his hands. 'But how is he here!'

'That doesn't matter,' insisted Emma.

Sebastian beamed. 'Are we going to listen to that man without hair again?' he said. 'He certainly had a lot to say. Is he your friend too?'

'Mr Clay? No, he's a teacher, and we have Mr Morecombe next, for maths.'

'Right,' said Sebastian. 'We have Mr Morecombe next, for maths.'

Oleg, Emma and Sebastian Cole crawled back into the roof, helped each other down on to the piano, and left the music room.

They were following the corridor towards their maths classroom when they came upon Elissa Goober. She was sitting on a plastic chair outside the headmistress's office. She was sobbing miserably into a tissue that was falling apart in her hands.

Sebastian Cole paused.

'Come on,' Oleg said. 'We'll be late for maths, and Morecombe's been acting weird lately. He'll go mental.'

'But she's upset!' Sebastian Cole insisted.

'But she's mean,' said Emma.

Sebastian Cole objected. 'One can be both mean and upset,' he said, raising a finger. 'In fact, it's often the meanest people that get the most upset. Why would a happy person waste time being mean? Look at her eyes, there's water coming out of them.'

'She's crying,' said Emma, trying not to feel sorry for a girl she was certain had never felt sorry for her.

'I'm right here,' said Elissa Goober, through her tears. 'I can hear you.' She blew her nose. It sounded like a bowl of soup being thrown at a wall.

'What happened to make that water come out of your eyes?' asked Sebastian.

'I was holding Rattie and he got away,' she said. Rattie supposedly lived in the laboratory but was more often found in Mrs Havers' hair. When he wasn't, students were sometimes allowed to play with him during breaktimes as long as they were careful. 'Everyone said I set him free on purpose but I really actually honestly didn't. And now they're going to call my mum and she's already angry and said I can't go and visit Dad on the weekend if I'm bad again.'

Sebastian Cole knelt down. 'What was this poor, sweet rodent wearing?'

'It wasn't wearing anything,' said Elissa. 'It's a rat.'

'A naked rat,' said Sebastian, nodding wisely. 'And what did it look like, apart from naked?'

'He's the shape of a pear,' said Elissa Goober. 'And he's brown and he has big yellow teeth and he smells like a toilet.' She burst into tears yet again. 'And now they're going to call my mum and she already said I had my last chance.'

Sebastian Cole flipped open the flap of his satchel and dug his hand in. He rooted around, deeper and deeper, until it looked as though he was about to fall into it. Finally, he found what he'd been looking for.

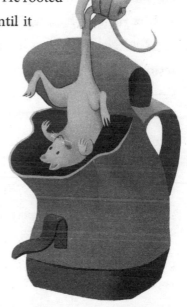

'Got it,' he said.

Oleg, who'd been hoping for even more warming ice-cream, was quite disappointed to see Sebastian pull out a lively, naked, pear-shaped, yellow-toothed rat.

Elissa Goober, on the other hand, was overjoyed.

'Thank you!' she said. 'Thank you, thank you, thank you!' She pulled Sebastian Cole into a fierce and sweaty hug. 'How did you find him? Where did you find him? How long have you had him?' Sebastian Cole shrugged. 'Oh, it doesn't matter. Thank you, Sebastian Cole.'

'Elissa Goober!' the headmistress called from her office. 'You may come in now.'

Elissa Goober wiped away her tears, straightened her blouse, and marched into the headmistress's office proudly holding the rat out before her.

'Sebastian?' asked Emma. 'You don't know any snowmen, do you?'

Oleg had no idea what she was talking about.

'Not currently,' answered Sebastian Cole. 'All the snowmen I've ever known are puddles now.'

11

The day felt like a thousand days squashed together. Every classroom was too cold, every lesson too boring. Emma and Oleg spent the hours distracting each other; they played boxes and hangman and pencil snap and sock swap and slaps.

Sebastian Cole proved himself to be a model student. He enthusiastically answered every question and wrote page after page of notes. When their teachers asked where he'd been on the first days, he claimed to have been hiking through the Himalayas in search of the abominable snowman. He told a long story involving an avalanche, a wild man, and spending four days living off one packet of chocolate biscuits.

Once half past three came around, Oleg and Emma were no closer to deciding what they ought to do about Sebastian Cole.

Emma thought that if he was here, then he was supposed to be here, and they should make the most of their time with him. Oleg didn't agree. He thought that whoever Sebastian was, and wherever he'd come from, he must have parents somewhere that were looking for him and they must be worried.

'I don't actually believe he has parents,' whispered Emma. 'He doesn't even know what Yorkshire puddings are.'

'But he said he doesn't tell lies.'

'Maybe it's a lie that he doesn't tell lies.'

Oleg suggested that they try to get him back into his spaceship, but when they raised the idea with Sebastian Cole he insisted that the ooberator was still broken and likely to stay broken for some time.

'You can't rush an ooberator,' he told them as though it was the most obvious thing in the world.

Kicking rocks and swishing sticks through the air, Oleg, Emma, and Sebastian Cole wandered towards the field over the motorway bridge.

They passed the newsagent.

And the singing ice-cream van.

The great glass library.

And the Red Lion pub.

Some houses were swaddled in flashing lights, giant

snowflakes, and glowing reindeer, while others stood quiet and empty as though they'd been forgotten.

Soon, the pavements were emptied of other schoolkids. Everyone else had run home to jump into hot showers or cradle mugs of tea. Oleg was uneasy. A shadow hung over the three of them.

'Emma,' he whispered. 'I think that car's following us.'

Emma glanced over his shoulder. A long, low black car was creeping up behind them. Its windows were such a dark grey that nothing inside the vehicle was visible.

'Why would it be following us?' Emma asked, not convinced.

'I don't know. But stop when I get to three.' He stuck three fingers out of a fist and counted as he folded them away. 'One, two, three.'

The three of them came to a halt.

As did the car behind them.

'It is after us,' said Oleg, struggling to breathe.

'Run!' screamed Emma.

The three of them ran full pelt towards the motorway bridge, until they realised then that if they went over, the car would just be waiting for them at the other side.

'Let's go over that fence,' said Emma. 'It's Mrs Fitzsimmons's house. Her dog'll bite anyone she doesn't know.'

They boosted each other over and dropped into a messy garden of frozen wildflowers, rusted rubbish, and an antique roll-top bathtub. A tubby dog with a bandana tied around its neck waddled out of the house. Emma crouched and let it lick her face. Oleg hid from the beast behind Sebastian Cole.

'There's a good girl,' Emma said. 'I'm afraid we have to get going.'

'Sorry, Mrs Fitzsimmons,' Oleg shouted, as they sprinted through the snow and leaped over the next fence.

The following garden was perfectly manicured. Somehow, the owner had kept the winter away entirely. A bright green oval lawn was hemmed with grey rocks, sweet-smelling water bubbled from a centaur-shaped fountain, and pristine flowers shone in their beds.

As they landed, a man with a red beard came running out of his house. He was in a ratty dressing gown and brandishing a broom like a sword.

'Halt!' the man shouted. 'Identify yourselves or be skewered.'

Oleg recognised him from times he'd come over to play poker with his dad and their friends. 'Hi, Mr Whitehouse!' he said. 'It's me.'

'Oleg?' said Mr Whitehouse. 'That you?' He lowered the broom. 'What on earth are you doing in my garden?'

'Long story,' said Oleg. 'Sorry, Mr Whitehouse, we have to run.'

'Tell your dad I said hello!' shouted Mr Whitehouse as the children disappeared over the next fence.

The garden after that was filled with ornate metal sculptures made from scrap metal. There were metal bears and metal bear cubs, giant insects, giant fish, replicas of the Eiffel Tower and Big Ben, and curious, rickety people who'd long since been swallowed by moss and covered with a thick coat of snow.

A bewildered man draped in several scarves emerged from the house. He wore a mask with a glass window in it, the kind you use to keep the sparks out of your eyes while working with metal.

'Sorry!' shouted Emma.

'We're not robbers,' explained Oleg.

'May all your wishes come true!' said Sebastian Cole.

That man wasn't in the least bit perturbed by the presence of three strange children. In fact, he was grateful for the excitement. He wished they'd have chosen to stay for a cup of tea. He found himself waving them goodbye.

The children threw themselves over the final hurdle.

They'd reached the end of the row of houses. All of them collapsed on to the ground, trying to catch their breath in the bitter cold, as their noses glowed red and crystals of ice formed on their eyelashes. They'd found themselves in a narrow alleyway with main roads at either end.

'I think I'm going to pass out,' said Oleg.

'Don't pass out,' advised Emma.

'Well it wouldn't be a choice.'

'Do you think we lost them?'

'There's no way they could have followed us over all those gardens.'

Suddenly, the car swerved around a corner. They glimpsed its blacked-out windows as one door swung open.

'Great,' said Emma.

They sprinted in the opposite direction, along the alleyway. None of them dared waste time turning around to see who was in pursuit. At first, heavy footsteps followed close behind. Then their pursuer seemed to change tactic and ran back to the car instead. Its motor roared.

'This way,' called Emma.

She led them through another alleyway, across a supermarket car park, and to a strip of shops that included an Indian restaurant, a Chinese restaurant, a nail salon, and a hairdresser for dogs.

Shanghai Palace, the Chinese restaurant, was owned by her mum's best friend. On busy nights her mum would help with deliveries, using Oliver's bicycle to save on petrol. That was the door she ushered them through, just as the big black car turned on to the street.

'Can we hide in your kitchen?' Emma asked a surprised Mrs So, without bothering to offer an explanation.

'Hide?' asked Mrs So. 'From who?'

'We're not entirely sure but we are sure that we need to hide from them.'

'In you go, in you go,' said Mrs So, who guessed that they were playing at some sort of game.

They rounded the counter and ducked into the kitchen. Hot woks spat oil and the rich, sticky smell of noodles floated into their noses. They found a spot in a metal cupboard packed with spices and jammed themselves together as best they could.

'This is exciting,' whispered Sebastian Cole.

'It's terrifying,' whispered Oleg.

'Shhhh,' whispered Emma.

Ten minutes later, Mrs So came to get them. She crouched down to their hiding place and opened the spice cupboard.

'What exactly have you got yourselves mixed up in?' she asked.

'Nothing!' Emma protested. 'We were walking home from school and that car just started following us. We ran through loads of gardens and it still managed to find us. Did someone come in?'

'A woman,' said Mrs So. 'At least, I think she was a woman. It was difficult to tell. She had a scarf wrapped around the bottom half of her face and a hat pulled over the top of it. Can you imagine?'

'What did she want?' asked Oleg.

'She wanted to know if three children had come in. I told her this is a restaurant, not a nursery. What would I want with three children? Not sure she believed me, but what was she going to do?' Mrs So shook her head. 'Do I need to call your mum, poppet?'

'Please don't, Mrs So,' said Emma. 'She'll only worry and she's probably at work. She's got so much on her plate at the moment, trying to get things ready for Christmas.'

Mrs So rolled her eyes. 'Then I won't,' she said. 'As long as you promise me to be careful.'

'Thank you, Mrs So. We'll all be unbelievably careful.'

'Little one, I don't like this at all.'

'I'm not little any more, Mrs So.'

'You're littler than me. Now run along. Call your mother if you need help, or your big brother at least.'

'We will!'

'Bye!'

Before they left, Mrs So made them each take a fortune cookie. She said that if they knew what was coming, it might be easier to prepare for.

*

They hurried on to the field that had been their original destination. The sun was starting to sink in the sky, leaving behind a luminous wash of pink. Cows were chewing snowflake-speckled grass. Electricity crackled through the wires overhead. Fortunately, no strange cars with dark windows appeared to chase them.

'Do you know who that could have been?' Oleg asked Sebastian Cole once he'd caught his breath.

Emma wrinkled her nose. 'Why are you so sure they were looking for Sebastian?'

'Because we've both lived here for ten years and no one's ever come chasing us in a car with blacked-out windows. Then suddenly he appears and it's like we're in an action film.'

'It's not his fault.'

'I know,' said Oleg. 'I'm sorry, I'm just scared.' He wasn't just scared because of the woman or the car. If he didn't know what was going on, then how was he supposed to know what to do?

'Oh, you shouldn't be scared,' said Sebastian Cole, beaming. 'Being scared is a terrible waste of time. Once a fortune teller told my mother she ought to prepare for blood to be shed in the coming week. My mother howled like a monkey in a washing machine! That's it, she told us, I'm done for! For a whole week, she refused to leave her bed. When she went to the toilet, she stubbed her toe, and a pinprick of blood was let loose. Oh, how we laughed. You see, being scared is just feeling pain before there is any pain to feel.'

'Yeah ...' said Emma, raising her eyebrows at Oleg. 'Plus we have a friend with a magic bag. If it can make ice-creams and rats then I'm sure it could make something that'll help us. Like a sword.'

'What would you do with a sword?' said Oleg.

Emma shrugged. 'I don't know. Throw it at someone?'

Oleg huffed. 'I just don't understand why someone would come looking for a person we'd made up,' he said.

'Pardon?' said Sebastian Cole.

'Sorry.'

'All is forgiven. It's possible you did make me up, even if that's not quite how it feels from here. I rather feel I made the two of you up. Perhaps I was feeling somewhat lonesome

✱ 86 *✱*

and decided to conjure up a little companionship.'

'My nan said we all started as an idea in someone's head,' said Oleg. 'Even me.'

'Where else would we start?' asked Sebastian Cole.

No one had an answer. They picked a path between the cows, dodging cushions of manure and snow-burdened stinging nettles, leaving behind three sets of winding footprints in the snow.

'We should hide,' said Oleg. 'In case the car's still waiting.'

'This way,' Emma called, running into a strip of trees at one side of the field. The cows lazily turned their heads to see what was going on. Losing interest, they turned back to the grass.

Through the trees and down a slope of dirt was a stream that ran out of a hole in a hill on the edge of town, wound through a forest, and disappeared into a concrete tunnel. The water was clear enough to drink.

Oleg had once found eight pound coins in the stream.

Together, they'd gone there to release a goldfish Emma had accidentally won at a travelling fair.

Without saying anything, the three of them set about gathering sticks, rocks, and old Coke cans. They found a perfect-sized piece of the stream and started working on a dam.

It was one of their favourite things to do, and it was the

perfect way of keeping themselves warm in the cold weather.

Sebastian Cole soon got the hang of it.

They built the dam higher and higher, weaving in thicker and thicker branches, and plugging the gaps with wads of fallen leaves. The water level rose. Water frothed and gushed over the dam, turning it into rapids. Tiny orange fish darted through the water like sparks of electricity.

Whenever anyone spotted a breach in the dam, they'd jump forward and patch it up. Over half an hour, they reinforced it until it became a bridge so strong a poodle could have wandered across it.

'That was fun,' Sebastian Cole said. 'But have you ever tried trout tickling? Truly, it is the sport of kings.'

From their blank looks, he could tell they'd never even heard of it.

'It's a way of catching fish,' Sebastian explained. 'Without a rod or a hook or bait.'

'Then how do you do it?' asked Oleg.

Sebastian Cole jumped into the stream to start his demonstration. 'You have to be really still,' he said. 'And terribly patient. First, you crouch and place your dainty hand palm-up, like this.'

He got on his knees and placed his hand on the bed of the stream.

'Then, you wait. And you wait. And you wait a little more. When a fish comes along, you gently stroke its belly like this.'

He mimed moving his hand back and forth.

'It tickles the fish so much that it is positively paralysed with laughter, at which point you're free to simply scoop the beast from the water!'

'Fish don't laugh,' Emma said, arms crossed.

'That's the stupidest thing I ever heard,' said Oleg.

They tried it anyway.

Oleg caught a blackened banana skin.

Emma caught half a bike wheel, the spokes warped as though it had smacked into something at high speed.

'This doesn't work at all,' she muttered, climbing out and shaking off droplets of icy water.

'Yes it does,' said Sebastian Cole. 'Look.'

He lifted his arm from the water to reveal a fish the size of a small guitar. The fish was the colour of pearls and it thrashed madly, spraying water and fishy spit through the air. Its eyes bulged and its gills rippled.

'Put it back!' screamed Emma.

Oleg, who had already run fifteen metres and was cowering under a willow tree, whimpered. He had his hands over his eyes. 'I don't like it,' he whispered.

'The poor thing isn't going to eat you,' remarked Sebastian

Cole. He lowered his arm back into the water and watched his catch slip away towards the concrete tunnel. 'Goodbye, sweet fish.'

Once they'd recovered from the shock, all three of them fell about laughing. Sebastian Cole wiped the slime off his arm with a dock leaf.

'Haven't you ever seen a fish before?' said Sebastian. 'Fish are dogs without legs that live in the water.'

'I've only seen their fingers,' said Oleg.

'You know fish fingers aren't actually the fingers of fish?' said Emma. 'You know fish don't actually have fingers?'

'I know,' said Oleg, turning red.

'Great,' said Emma, patting her burbling belly. 'Now I'm hungry.'

'Me too.'

They snacked on their fortune cookies while sitting on the bank of the brook. One by one, they read out their fortunes.

Oleg's said: *Relax and take a bath, the world won't end today.*

Emma's said: *There is being brave and there is being stupid, be careful not to get the two mixed up.*

And Sebastian Cole's said: *To be alive is a wonderful adventure, make every second count.*

12

I t was decided that Emma's mum was more likely to accept an unexpected guest than Oleg's dad, even though Oleg's dad would probably be asleep. The risk was that whenever Oleg's dad was awake, he was extremely grumpy about not being asleep, and would take it out on anyone who happened to be nearby.

'Mum!' Emma called as they came in through the patio doors. 'I've got friends over!'

But her mum was out working at an all-night café in the middle of town, where nurses and firemen and security guards on nightshifts went for cups of sweet tea and big greasy breakfasts.

'Your mum speaks very quietly,' said Sebastian Cole, swivelling his head to try and catch a glimpse of his new friend's guardian.

'She's not here,' explained Emma. 'She's at work and

she'll probably be gone all night.'

'Ah,' said Sebastian. 'Is she a bat-catcher?'

'No, she makes coffee.'

'Why?' asked Sebastian. 'Wouldn't she rather be here?'

Emma gave him a look as if to say: please stop talking. 'Of course she'd rather be here,' she said. 'But she's got to work.'

Sebastian nodded. 'She's got to make coffee otherwise terrible things happen.'

'Sort of,' sighed Emma.

They found her brother, Oliver, in the kitchen. He was wearing a chequered apron and a tall paper hat, and his cheeks were dusty with flour.

Emma clicked the kettle on for tea.

Her brother ground salt and pepper into a large metal bowl, tore up some leaves and threw them in, then leaned into his concoction and inhaled. He sighed. He was pleased with what he smelled.

'Try this,' said Oliver, waving Emma over. 'It's fresh tagliatelle pasta with mint.' He winked. 'I found the mint growing in Mrs Fitzsimmons's garden and she let me take as much as I wanted.'

'You made the pasta?' Oleg asked.

Oliver beamed. 'Rolled it out myself.'

They stood around the bowl and each slurped up strands

of the rich, buttery pasta.

'This is the best pasta I've ever had,' said Sebastian Cole.

'It's the first pasta you've ever had,' said Oleg.

And they all laughed, except for Oliver, who was beginning to wonder where this new boy had come from. Were there places without pasta? If there were, it sounded like the perfect business opportunity.

Not wanting to arouse suspicion, Emma told him they'd be going out to the shed. 'To do homework,' she added. 'We have a lot of homework to be getting on with.'

The garden shed was packed with rusty rakes, punctured footballs, half-empty tins of paint, and machine parts so old that no one could remember what they belonged to.

Cobwebs hung from the corners.

Wellies caked in mud were piled on ancient raincoats and paint-splattered sheets.

The three of them sat on upturned buckets.

Emma poured tea out of a pot she'd filled, into mismatched mugs Oleg had grabbed from the cupboard. They added spoonfuls of sugar and splashes of milk.

'What do we do now?' asked Emma, rolling her mug between her hands.

'I'm not sure,' said Oleg. 'But Sebastian's obviously in danger. Maybe it's best if he stays here tomorrow.'

'I'm coming with you to see the man who loves talking about kings!' Sebastian insisted. 'I'm not sitting around somewhere on my own. That would be several thousand times more dangerous. What's best for all of us is remaining incredibly close and making sure to scream like wet pandas if anyone comes.'

'But what if they come to school?'

'Then we shall be forced to concoct a plan,' said Sebastian. 'I am an expert at concocting plans.'

They sipped their teas.

'I still don't get who they could be,' said Oleg. 'Who would want to catch a boy that only appeared this morning?'

'I think we should go and see the groundskeeper,' Emma said.

Oleg was used to his friend coming up with strange plans but this one made no sense. 'Why would we go and see the gardener?' he said. 'What does he have to do with Sebastian?'

'Maybe they're connected,' said Emma. 'I told my mum about our den, and she told me that the cowboy gardener had been at our school when she was. Then I tried to work out the maths: my mum was at school forty years ago. She said he was about eighty then. That would make him one hundred and twenty today.'

'That's impossible,' said Oleg.

'Exactly,' replied Emma. 'Just like Sebastian.'

'So you think the school groundskeeper is one hundred and twenty years old, so we should ask him what to do with the boy who appeared in our den?'

'Okay,' said Emma. 'Let's go with your plan then.'

'But I don't have a plan.'

Emma stuck out her tongue. 'Exactly.'

Oleg swallowed. He may not have had a plan, but he did have a growing sense that something very bad was about to happen.

✳

They found the groundskeeper in his shed at the far end of the field. It was a one-room building made of metal sheets, with circular windows that drew long beams of orange light on the snow.

'Should we knock?' asked Emma.

'Maybe we should go home,' Oleg whispered. 'He's a stranger. Remember stranger danger?'

'He's not a stranger,' Emma whispered back. 'He works at school. They don't let strangers work at school.'

'I can hear you,' the groundskeeper whispered through the

door. 'And I applaud your caution. Very sensible.'

The door swung open to reveal the groundskeeper standing in a pair of muddy overalls with a cowboy hat perched on top of his head. A strand of straw was clamped in one corner of his mouth.

'I'm Sebastian Cole,' said Sebastian, thrusting out his hand. 'But you already know that.'

Emma and Oleg rolled their eyes.

'Best come in, Sebastian Cole,' said the groundskeeper. 'It's chilly out there and I've seen strange things about lately.'

They followed the cowboy gardener into his shed. It was a cosy but cluttered room, piled high with dusty books. The children took seats on stacks of old novels. A pyramid of logs blazed in an open fire.

From a pot that was bubbling over the flames, the groundskeeper filled three mugs with hot chocolate and passed them out to the children. It didn't taste like any chocolate Oleg had tried before. It was a rich, dark taste that stretched from his toes to his ears and made him feel as though he'd gone back to being five years old.

The groundskeeper found a bucket for himself, tipped it over, and sat. He nodded at the three children in turn. There was nothing menacing about him but something about his presence unsettled Oleg.

'Drink up,' said the caretaker. 'It'll keep you warm. Now tell me, what brings you here on a night like this?'

Emma wasn't sure how to start. She knew it would be rude to ask about his age and she had no idea how to explain who Sebastian really was. Should she be honest? What if he thought they were trying to play a trick on him?

She sipped her drink and felt the hot chocolate calm her head. 'We were wondering how much you might know about things that don't make sense,' she said.

The caretaker didn't reply straight away. He closed his eyes, sipped from his mug, chewed on his piece of grass, then spoke. 'When was the last time you looked at the sky?' he asked.

None of them answered.

What did the sky have to do with anything?

The caretaker took off his cowboy hat and held it pressed to his chest, looking from face to face. Finally, he pulled the piece of straw from his mouth and aimed it at Sebastian Cole.

'Go on then,' he said. 'Which one of you imagined him?'

'Neither of us,' Oleg said, far too quickly. 'As you can see, he's very unimaginary. He even has a smell.' He wasn't sure why but he felt certain that they shouldn't admit he had appeared out of nowhere, even if Emma thought it could help. It seemed like a risky thing to tell an adult.

'I do not have a smell,' said Sebastian Cole, twisting round to get a whiff of his own shoulder.

'Of course you have a smell,' said Emma. 'Everything has a smell. And yes, we did imagine him. We were inventing new friends and this one appeared in our den.'

'It's a dangerous game,' said the groundskeeper. 'Meddling with the way things are. The world isn't kind to dreams.'

'I am neither a dangerous game nor a dream,' said Sebastian, sticking out his chin. 'I am double-jointed and capable of extraordinary cartwheels.'

'His name's Sebastian Cole,' said Emma.

'But you already know that,' said Oleg.

They both fell into raucous laughter while the groundskeeper watched on, confused. 'This is no laughing matter,' he said. 'Do you know what they'll do to him if they catch him?'

Their laughter fell away.

'If who catches him?'

'The ones tasked with keeping the rabbits in the hats! The keepers of the order! They'll take him to a tiny white room, in a huge grey building, and leave him there, ignored, until he fades to nothing. The forgotten folk disappear faster than shooting stars. We need to be noticed, we need to be seen, we need to be heard.'

'What do you mean "we"?' Oleg interjected. 'And why would anyone care if Sebastian existed?'

'Just listen.' The groundskeeper pulled an old-fashioned radio from below his chair and extended the antenna. After twisting the dial through a crackle of white noise, he landed on a station and a voice filled the room.

'This is your seven o'clock evening news broadcast,' said the voice. 'We have reports coming in from the Isle of Skye that a number of families have woken up to find large, tropical trees occupying their kitchens and living rooms. It is unclear yet where these trees have come from or how they have managed to survive in such conditions. We'll have more on this story as it comes in.

'In other news, Janet Cleaver of Birdhall, Nebraska has won the jackpot at her bingo hall three days running. When interviewed about her wins, Mrs Cleaver said that she was over the moon, and that things like this simply never happened to her.'

The groundskeeper turned the radio off.

'What has that got to do with Sebastian?' asked Emma.

The groundskeeper tapped the side of his head. 'Just think about it,' he said. 'The world is built of dominos.'

'It's made of pizza?' asked Emma.

'Good,' said Sebastian Cole. 'I've always wanted to eat a pizza.'

'No!' shouted the groundskeeper. 'I'm not talking about pizza, what's wrong with you? I'm talking about dominos. Where one falls and the others fall too. One tiny change can trigger a thousand larger changes. One impossible thing can lead to an impossible world.'

The three children blinked at him uncertainly.

Suddenly, his face tightened up, as though a startling thought had come into his head. He looked afraid. He jumped to his feet, knocking over his mug and spilling hot chocolate the length of the cabin.

'I've said enough,' the groundskeeper said. 'You ought to be going.'

The caretaker then ushered them hurriedly out of the shed and slammed the door shut behind them.

'Everything's getting weirder and weirder,' said Emma, puzzled. 'What was he talking about?'

'Pizza,' said Sebastian Cole, curiously nudging a pile of snow with his foot as though to test whether it was made of bread and molten cheese.

'Maybe he's Sebastian's dad,' suggested Oleg.

'My dad is not a cowboy gardener,' said Sebastian. 'He's a

successful businessman with tremendously shiny shoes. He runs a kitchen supply firm that stretches from Japan to the other side of Japan.'

'He made it sound like Sebastian shouldn't be here,' said Oleg. 'Like those people are going to keep coming for him.'

'Well he is here,' said Emma. 'And we're not going to let them come for him.'

'We don't even know who they are!'

'We know the caretaker knows more than he told us, otherwise he wouldn't have made us leave so quickly. We just need to get him to tell us everything.'

'But how?' asked Oleg.

'We could torture him,' said Sebastian Cole. 'With sticks or fire.'

Emma and Oleg stared at him.

'I was joking,' explained Sebastian. 'It was just a joke, like the one you made earlier.' He looked sadly at his hands. 'I see now that it has failed.'

'No,' said Oleg, feeling bad for the strange boy who spoke like an alien. 'It was a good joke.'

Back in Emma's shed, they played Snap until the sky outside got so dark that Oleg said he ought to go. He felt left out to be the only one not sleeping over but knew that asking to spend a school night at someone else's house would probably mean getting loudly shouted at. There was always the option of staying out without asking, but if Oleg's dad happened to wake up while he was gone, the shouting would be even louder.

'I should go,' Oleg said. 'If Dad wakes up and I'm not there, he'll be angry.'

'Why would he be asleep already?' asked Sebastian Cole.

'All he does is sleep,' explained Oleg.

'Does he have a disease?'

'No,' said Oleg. 'He just doesn't get excited any more.'

Sebastian looked confused.

The three of them stepped out of the shed.

'Look,' said Oleg, pointing at the grass under their feet.

The lawn had been ploughed clear of snow.

'How kind,' said Sebastian Cole. 'I suppose we really shouldn't torture him after all.'

13

That night, Oleg lay in bed trying to figure out exactly what was going on. The cold was making it impossible to sleep, as was the question of Sebastian Cole and the unexplained car and the groundskeeper and the goat that was apparently wandering around the school grounds, wreaking havoc.

Maybe he hadn't made Sebastian Cole up at all, he thought. Maybe Sebastian wasn't really called Sebastian and he was just a boy on the run for some terrible crime. Maybe he overheard Oleg talking to Mr Morecombe and stole the name. Maybe he and Emma would be arrested for harbouring a fugitive.

Or maybe he was accidentally granted a wish or he'd accidentally used a magic pen or magic paper. In which case, the world didn't work quite the way he thought it did, and he wouldn't mind knowing exactly what the new rules were.

He knew there had to be a simple, logical explanation, but no matter how hard he thought, he couldn't find it.

His tummy moaned.

For dinner, all he'd had was a microwave lasagne. It had tasted strange and sugary and he wished he had had some more of the mint pasta.

Oleg had tried to cook properly but his attempts had almost always been disastrous. There had been chewy pucks of meat in watery sauces, chicken that was pink inside and forced him to take two days off school, and a kind of eggy cake that exploded out of the oven and left long burn marks on the ceiling and walls.

Before his dad had been lost to the world of sleep, they would make big batches of pierogi every Sunday. They would make the dough, roll it out, and stamp out circles. Each circle would have filling spooned in, be folded shut, and sealed with little thumb crimps.

Usually, they'd fill them with mince or potato or cabbage. Sometimes they experimented. There had been chilli pierogi and tuna pierogi and even pierogi filled with chunks of chocolate that tasted so strange they ate one each then ordered Indian food.

They'd make heaps and heaps of pierogi and freeze them for the week ahead. Then, whenever anyone was hungry, they'd pluck a few out, boil them for a second, fry them in butter, and eat them with great clumps of sour cream and chopped spring onion. Even if Oleg sometimes forgot how Poland had felt, he never forgot how it tasted, and each mouthful felt like being somewhere warm and safe. He felt closest to his dad while they were eating together. Lately it had felt like his dad was standing on the other side of the ocean.

Would Christmas pass by like any other day?

Looking out of his window at the moon, Oleg remembered what the caretaker had said. 'When was the last time you looked at the sky?' Why would he have asked that?

Oleg looked and looked.

And looked.

And looked.

Something fizzed, like a glittering silver asterisk.

And something huge, red, and blazing shot across the sky.

He blinked. Everything was stationary again.

Oleg guessed it was a comet or a shooting star, though he'd never seen anything that bright burn across the sky at night. He'd seen a shooting star once before and used it to wish for a suit of armour that had never arrived. Since then, he hadn't cared much about shooting stars or wishes.

He heard something coming from above. It sounded like a handful of rocks being scattered on the ceiling.

Grandma was awake.

She often started going at her typewriter at odd hours. She'd once told him inspiration always struck whenever was least convenient. It meant that she sometimes wound up sleeping whole days through, the nights lost to imaginary worlds. In the dark of the attic, it probably didn't much matter whether it was day or night anyway.

Wanting someone to talk to, Oleg kicked off his duvet and went up to the attic. The light was on and Grandma was nibbling on a wedge of cheese and taking sips from a mug the size of a baby's head. She had her own kettle in the attic, as well as a miniature fridge where she chiefly kept milk and cheese and large, out-of-date pots of chocolate mousse.

'Hi, Grandma,' he said.

She stopped chewing and typing and turned to her grandson, smiling.

'Good morning,' she said.

'It's not morning,' explained Oleg. 'I think it's about midnight.'

'Well, it'll be morning soon enough. Come and sit up here.' Grandma patted an old trombone case propped up beside her. Oleg did as he was told. 'You have something on your mind,' Grandma said.

'Yes,' admitted Oleg.

'Something scary but not altogether terrible.'

'You're right,' said Oleg. 'Can I ask you something?'

'It never hurts to ask.'

'Have you ever heard of someone appearing out of nowhere? I don't mean like a baby, I mean like a whole person just appearing without any reason or anything.'

Grandma thought.

And thought.

She finished her tea.

And her cheese.

'See that book over there?' she said, pointing to one corner of the crowded attic. 'The one with the purple cover. Bring that over to me, please.'

Oleg scrambled past overflowing cardboard boxes and nearly toppled a precarious stack of video tapes trying to get it. Once he had the book, he blew dust off the cover to reveal the title: *Unexplained Mysteries of the World*. He passed it to Grandma.

'Of course,' Grandma said, 'many have heard of unexplained disappearance, but not so many have heard of unexplained appearance. Nevertheless, it happens. Have you ever heard of the green children of Woolpit?' Oleg told her he hadn't. 'Theirs is one of the first recorded cases of unexplained appearance. Listen to this.'

She rifled through the book until she came to the page she was looking for, cleared her throat, and started reading.

'On a summer afternoon, in the year 1073, two children, a boy and a girl, appeared in the village of Woolpit. They were found in one of the big stone pits that the villagers used to trap wolves. The children both had bright green skin, spoke in their own bizarre language, and would only eat raw broad beans.

'Once they'd learned English, they said they came from a land where the sun never rose or set and everything was green. They said that they'd been looking after cows, when they followed one into a cave and emerged in our world.

'Where the children had come from was never discovered for sure, though it has been suggested that they fell through from a nearby world, climbed out of an imagination, or were accidentally dropped to earth by passing aliens. Many believe that they escaped from one of the earliest written stories. Stories were so infrequently written down back then, that the children panicked to find themselves appearing in one, and fled the pages of the book.

'Anyhow, the children ended up spending their lives working as servants in a rich house. They never got on well with normal people, remaining grumpy and quiet their entire lives.

'And that,' concluded Grandma, 'is the story of the green twins of Woolpit.'

'That can't be true,' said Oleg.

'Of course it's true. The tale has been verified. It was written about by two writers who lived at the time, Ralph of Coggeshall and William of Newburgh.'

'But why would it happen?'

'Why would anything happen? The universe came out of nothing, why shouldn't people? Sometimes, reality isn't as stable as we think it is. There are times when the unlikeliest things happen, one after the other.'

Grandma sighed. 'Of course,' she said, 'most cases like these are made to disappear as quickly as they appeared. They are too disruptive otherwise; there's too much paperwork involved.'

'Made to disappear how?' Oleg asked, thinking of the car with the blacked-out windows.

'That is information I have never been privy to, though of course I hear whispers. The problem with whispers, dear boy, is that they can be terribly difficult to make out.'

'Grandma?'

'What is it?'

'What would you do if you found a person who had unexpectedly appeared?'

'I would take very good care of him,' said Grandma. 'Now I think it's time for bed.'

It wasn't until Oleg's head hit the pillow that he realised he'd never told Grandma it was a him. He was struck again by the feeling that adults had access to far more information than was fair. How did they know which lumps and bumps to worry about? How did they know which buttons to press on the washing machine and how to get ketchup off a shirt, and why it is that sometimes people appear out of nowhere?

14

The next morning, Emma and Sebastian left home early to avoid having to explain their unplanned sleepover to Emma's mum. Neither of them had got much sleep. Sebastian, it turned out, was far too excitable to even come close to dozing off. He'd spent the whole night walking around the house, picking things up and putting them back down.

He'd been amazed by Emma's fossil collection.

And the spoons in the cutlery drawer.

The decades-old Christmas decorations.

And the ten-year-old Nintendo.

He dipped his tongue into various sauces and spices.

He spoke to the spiders and the moths.

He flicked through every celebrity gossip magazine he could find.

'Look at her!' he'd say. 'What a fabulous dress, like a

thousand glimmering cobwebs spun together!'

When she introduced Sebastian to Pip, the two of them immediately set to work on an old puzzle of the Eiffel Tower. Pip fell asleep face-first on France's most famous monument and Emma ended up carrying him to bed.

And then, somehow, morning had come and Sebastian Cole had just as much energy as ever. Emma, on the other hand, felt as though she could topple over and fall asleep at any second. The cold wasn't helping. It had settled in every available space and made itself impossible to escape. As excited as she was over the appearance of a new friend, it was impossible to ignore the gnawing hunger in her belly and the chill in her fingers. She wasn't in the mood to think about mysterious cowboy gardeners or prowling cars.

She let loose a wide yawn as they arrived at the school. It was almost deserted, except for a few cars and the kids that came in early to swim.

Entering the form room, they froze.

A head was bobbing about behind the desk. It wasn't Mr Clay. The hair was too silver and too sparse. They stood for a while, waiting. Then Mr Morecombe rose up from where he'd been fumbling with something. He jumped when he saw them, his cheeks lighting up red, as he pressed an open bag to his chest.

'What are you doing?' Emma asked.

'What do you mean, what am I doing?' said Mr Morecombe. 'I'm a teacher.'

'But you're not *our* teacher, sir.'

'I do not have to explain myself to you, young lady.' He jabbed a finger in her direction. 'Perhaps you ought to explain yourself. What is it that you are doing here?'

'We're allowed to come in early and work if we want to.'

'Who is that boy?'

'I'm Sebastian Cole,' said Sebastian. 'But you already know that.'

Mr Morecombe frowned. 'How would I possibly already know that?'

Sebastian wasn't sure what to say.

'I think it's best if we all forget we saw each other,' said Mr Morecombe.

'But I have a remarkable memory,' announced Sebastian Cole. 'I can remember things that haven't even happened. I once remembered being bitten by a hammerhead shark with teeth like knives but it turned out I'd only been eating tomato soup.'

'Shh,' said Emma.

'Yes,' said Mr Morecombe. 'Listen to your friend, boy – shh.' He swept out of the room.

'That was weird,' said Emma.

'Was it?' asked Sebastian Cole, who wouldn't know weird if it climbed out of a toilet bowl dressed as an apricot and started barking like a dog.

They searched behind the desk for any clues as to what the teacher might have been doing. They found absolutely nothing.

15

O leg's walk to school wasn't without incident either. He walked the way he always walked, through the quieter alleys and across the triangle of grass where local kids played football.

Snow caked his shoes.

The sky shook off its last few night-time clouds and promised another day of brain-zapping cold. He wasn't looking forward to school but he wanted to get to the bottom of Sebastian Cole. He was planning to ask whether or not Sebastian liked raw beans and if he'd ever turned green or herded any cows through any caves. The words of the cowboy gardener echoed in his head: *one impossible thing can lead to an impossible world.* If you never knew what was going to happen next, thought Oleg, the world would be even more terrifying than it already was. You might be walking to school and have a piano fall on your head. You might be washing your hands when the water turns to scalding lava.

Coming off the snow-covered grass, he turned left towards the library.

That was when he saw it up ahead.

The van was so reflective that you almost couldn't see that it was there. It simply mirrored the snow-heaped streets. Only eight thick black wheels gave away the fact that it was a vehicle. There was no licence plate, no lights, no back door.

Cautiously, Oleg crossed the road.

He kept his eye on the van as he sidled along.

It wasn't the blacked-out car from the day before but it almost certainly wasn't a plumber or a decorator either. It looked like something that had come from the future.

Usually, Oleg walked the way he walked so as to be alone. That morning, he wished more than anything that some form of adult would come out of a nearby house. It could have been anyone and he wouldn't have minded, even doddery Mrs Phipps or old Mr Carmichael and the one-eyed ferret he kept on a lead.

As he was about to cross the kerb, Oleg fell.

When he opened his eyes, he was somewhere else entirely.

He guessed from the size it was the inside of the van, though he had no idea how he would have got in there. All he could see were four ceiling corners and a painfully bright white light that was making purple stars dance past his eyes.

His stomach bounced about behind his belly button as though he were riding a rollercoaster.

A face loomed over his. Half of the face was covered by a mask, the nose curved into a beak and the edges papered with feathers. It looked like something that belonged in a ballroom, not in a van parked halfway up the road to school. The eyes behind the mask were electric blue. They stared accusingly down at Oleg.

'Have you seen this boy?' the crow asked, holding a fuzzy photo of Sebastian Cole up to Oleg's face. The voice sounded like it was coming from a woman, but a woman who had been munching rocks and sand.

'No,' said Oleg with a whimper.

'When did you see him?'

'I've never seen him.'

The mask moved closer to his face. Up close, he saw that the eyes were spiderwebbed with red veins as though the woman hadn't slept for days. 'I am not going to ask twice,' she said.

Oleg fought to sit up but no part of his body would respond. Only his eyes and mouth were free to move. What had happened to him? 'What have you done to me?' he demanded to know.

'You have not been harmed in any way,' said the crow. 'I only need you to co-operate. When did this boy arrive at your school?'

'I don't know any boy.'

'You know many boys.'

'Not the one you want.'

'How did he get to be here?'

'Bus?'

'Don't be smart with me.'

'I don't know who you're talking about.'

Oleg felt as though the air had been sucked out of his chest.

'We've had reports of a confabulatory activity in the area,' said the crow. 'This is serious. While B612 is passing by, the fabric of everything is being thrown into disarray.'

Oleg had no idea what she was talking about. The mask moved so close to his face that the beak touched his own nose. He could smell bleach and spent matches. 'Do you know what happens when the line between reality and unreality gets blurred?' it said. 'We have to pick up the pieces, in case they get stepped on, and you are currently in possession of the largest piece. If we do not have him by tomorrow, we will have to move in with force, and we will not be gentle.'

'He didn't do anything wrong!' exclaimed Oleg.

And then he closed his eyes and screamed.

When he opened his eyes again he was standing back on the pavement near the triangle of grass, his heart launching itself against his ribs as though it were trying to escape. That didn't happen, he told himself. *That didn't happen, that didn't happen.*

Oleg sprinted the rest of the way to school and burst into the form room. He was still early. The only other people inside were Emma and Sebastian Cole, who were playing noughts and crosses at a table in the corner.

They panicked when they saw the look on his face.

'What is it?' asked Emma.

'I think the groundskeeper was right,' Oleg replied. 'Someone really is coming for Sebastian.'

He went on to explain the mirror van and the face in the crow mask and not being able to move. Both Emma and Sebastian shivered. They were sure of one thing: for now, school had to be the safest place. There was no way the teachers would let some masked crow-woman rampage through the corridors and haul a student away. Would they?

16

$\mathcal{E}$verything in school was so normal that Oleg wanted to scream. *The boy next to me crash-landed in a spaceship! I was kidnapped in the world's shiniest van! Goat! Crow! Cowboy! Ice-creams appearing out of a bag!*

Emma, on the other hand, didn't have quite so much trouble with what was going on. This was no weirder than the snowmen, and really, if you thought about it, were snowmen and strange boys all that much weirder than rainbows or killer whales or those plants that catch bugs in their mouths?

She'd seen a ghost once, on holiday in Cornwall. It had been a girl of about her age who said she'd fallen into a well three hundred years earlier. She wasn't scary, she didn't moan or groan or clank chains, and she didn't look like a sheet with two holes cut out of it for eyes either. *So there's a place other than this one?* Emma had asked. *Oh, yes,* the girl had said. *Far more places.* And from then on Emma had rarely been surprised. *If there were ghosts,* she reasoned, *there could be almost anything.*

✻

The rest of 6Y were back to playing their game of trying to divert Mr Clay's attention away from anything that resembled work.

'Sir?' asked Scott Ballantine. 'How big is the biggest foot on earth?'

'What's a Nebuchadnezzar?' asked Callie Jones.

'Theoretically, sir, how would you catch a mongoose?'

'Please,' said Mr Clay. 'I've given you worksheets and I'd appreciate it if you all settled down and got on with them.'

There were three whole minutes before the questions started up again.

'How did medieval people cut their fingernails?'

'Does the queen own the clouds?'

'How much does a horse cost?'

Mr Clay raised his hands to end the questions, which was when the headmistress launched herself through the door. She was dressed in sharp clothes that looked as though they'd been made out of thin sheets of metal. Her hair was slicked back into a sleek helmet.

She marched to the front of the classroom and slammed a blue folder down on the desk. Mr Clay jumped in his seat.

'Do you know what this is?' she said. Mr Clay said nothing. 'This is a register.' She jabbed it with a bony finger. 'And this is the third day you've failed to complete one. I have asked you and I have asked you again. I will not repeat myself once more.'

Mr Clay was frozen in place.

'What happens if a fire engulfs the school, Mr Clay? Which of us should rush into the flames to rescue a child that might be home sick? How will we know who's at home and who's here?'

'I … I …' stuttered Mr Clay. His bottom lip was quivering.

'You put our lives and the lives of the children in jeopardy when you fail to follow protocol. Do I make myself clear?'

'Yes.'

'This is your final warning. If you fail to take even one more register, you will be escorted out of this school. I will not have the lives I am tasked with protecting put in danger because you cannot be bothered to read off a list of names.'

The headmistress charged out of the room. The air she left behind felt ten degrees cooler than it had before she'd passed through it.

Mr Clay looked so dejected that 6Y couldn't help but feel

sorry for him. He sat at his desk with his head in his hands and stared sadly into an empty coffee mug.

'Sir?' asked Scott Ballantine. 'How come you never did the register?'

'I meant to,' answered Mr Clay. 'But it kept disappearing. I looked everywhere for it but it was never there.'

'It's okay, sir,' said Ora. 'We'll make sure you do the next one.'

'Thank you, Ora,' said Mr Clay, lifting his head and faintly smiling. 'That would be very helpful.'

At breaktime, Oleg, Emma, and Sebastian Cole went up to the roof to check for shiny vans in the streets. Oleg was worried that the one he'd seen could have been the first of many, and that they were planning to close in on the school and steal Sebastian Cole away.

'There's no way I'm walking home,' said Oleg. 'There could be more of those vans waiting to grab me again. If they catch Sebastian, there's no way we'd get him back. They could take him anywhere.'

He shuddered, remembering the masked face, and wondering where they could go for help. There was no way he could reach his nan, and the groundskeeper had seemed to want them out of his cabin as quickly as possible.

'Then what do we do?' said Emma.

'We could sleep up here for now. If we stay behind the generators, they might keep us warm.'

They glanced at each other.

It was decided.

Emma called to tell her mum she was staying at Oleg's and Oleg left a voicemail for his dad saying he was staying at Emma's. Hopefully, both parents would be too preoccupied to check their alibis.

17

*S*towing away in school was not a difficult task to accomplish. At the end of the day, the three of them simply climbed up to their spot on the roof and watched the teachers' cars purr out of the car park one by one.

When they were certain they were on their own, they finally relaxed, and started discussing things that could take their minds off the situation at hand.

Sebastian Cole wanted to know all about school. What did they get at the end? How long did they stay for? Could you stay for ever if you wanted? Did you learn about robots? And whales? What about teeth?

'And what was everyone doing just now?' he asked. 'We were supposed to be writing about King Henry the Eighth but the boy who smells of brie was writing about something called Mercurial Vapor football boots.'

'They were writing Christmas lists,' explained Oleg. 'You write down what you want for Christmas and then your parents get it for you.'

Sebastian nodded. 'And you didn't write one because there's nothing in the world that you want.'

Oleg didn't correct him. He hadn't written a list for the last two years and neither had Emma. They'd stopped seeing the point.

They asked him about his school but Sebastian said he couldn't remember much of it.

'I think it smelled of plasticine,' he suggested, and they all agreed that every school they'd ever been in had smelled like plasticine. They tried to list as many animals beginning with P as they could. They played I-Spy until everything spy-able had been spied.

The sky slid from blue to orange to pink.

Emma and Oleg put on their hats and Sebastian Cole unravelled his scarf from his neck so the three of them could sit with it over their laps.

'Where am I going to live?' asked Sebastian Cole, a hint of sadness in his voice. 'I'm not sure I can intrude on your hospitality for ever. I've been thinking about tinkering with the ooberator but tinkering with an ooberator's like tinkering with a hurricane. I like it here, don't think that I don't, but it seems as though someone isn't desperately keen on my presence.'

Emma cleared her throat.

'There are lots of books where people live in forests,' she said. 'You can build a treehouse and have a slide and a swing and a pet monkey who plays chess.'

'And we can visit whenever we want,' added Oleg. 'We could even move there when we're older and work from home on computers.'

'You could build lots of treehouses in nearby trees.'

'And then connect them all with rope bridges.'

'Like a whole city in the trees.'

'That sounds nice,' sighed Sebastian Cole. 'I do think I'd like that. And I'll come to this school every single day and listen to the bald man talk.'

'Um,' said Oleg. 'But we're going to be leaving this year.'

'Really? Where will you be going?'

Oleg looked at Emma and Emma looked away.

'We don't know yet,' they said in unison.

Oleg yawned which made Emma yawn which made Sebastian yawn.

Sebastian opened his bag and carefully pulled a very long, thin rod out of it. He passed it to Oleg.

'What's it for?' asked Oleg, wiggling it experimentally in the air.

'Whatever it is,' said Emma, 'hold it still or you'll have someone's eye out.'

Sebastian Cole produced another rod and gave it to Emma, then tugged out an unbelievably large square of blue fabric.

'It's a double-insulated, water-cooled, three-man mountain tent,' he said. 'Or it will be when we get it set up.'

Together, they set up the tent. It took longer than the instructions said it would, which, as the instructions were written in Welsh, was not enormously surprising.

'I need to get one of those bags,' said Emma when they were done.

'Me too,' said Oleg.

They piled into the tent and feasted on various other things that Sebastian's bag produced. There were chicken nuggets and chips, buttery toast and thick-cut crisps, meat pies, samosas, pasties, and big plates of sloppy noodles.

'That was too much food,' said Oleg when they were done. 'I think my belly button's disappeared.'

But there was enough space for ice-cream, and also for hot chocolate, because it is a well-known fact that there are certain corners of the stomach reserved entirely for those two substances.

Full of food and exhausted with excitement, Oleg, Emma, and Sebastian Cole felt their arms and legs growing heavy and their eyes sliding shut.

As the three children fell slowly asleep in a tent on the roof of their school …

Emma's mum served huge mugs of coffee in the night café.

Oliver dreamed of gleaming cutlery.

Pip lay asleep on an open book.

Grandpa Lewis shovelled in his last slice of ham.

Oleg's dad snored like a tractor engine on the sofa.

And Grandma sat in the attic, picking out the beginnings of a marvellous adventure on her typewriter.

18

That night, it wasn't the cold that woke Emma up, but a curious grumbling sound coming from somewhere down below.

She unzipped the tent and winced as a wave of ice-cold air bit into her face.

She leaned forward.

She gasped.

There was a snowman in the school car park, trudging around in circles, twitching its twig arms as though in a panic. Snow fell in whirls, lit by the pale yellow glow of the moon.

So, Emma thought, *there really were snowmen and I really did see them and they're really not going to get away this time.*

She put on her shoes and pulled on her hat.

Carefully, she shimmied down one of the drainpipes that linked the roof to the ground. Her shoes crunched in the snow but the snowman didn't seem to notice. It carried on waddling aimlessly around, flailing its arms and moaning like a child in a tantrum.

As she took a few steps closer, Emma realised why the snowman hadn't seen her approach: it had no eyes.

'Hello?' called Emma, her heart tingling behind her ribs. 'Can you hear me?'

The snowman froze.

'Who said that?' it asked.

'I did,' repeated Emma, stepping forward.

The snowman's carrot nose twitched. 'And does I have eyes?'

Emma was confused for a moment before she realised what was being asked. She laughed. 'Yes,' she said. 'I have eyes. Two of them.'

'There's no need to brag,' said the snowman. 'Now would you use your two eyes to help me find mine? They've fallen out and everyone else has gone on without me.'

'Of course,' said Emma.

She fell to her knees in the snow and felt around the icy ground with her hands. They burned with pain, though she tried her best to ignore it. She wanted to help the snowman, at least partly because then he might be able to tell her something about what was going on.

And Emma knew how it felt to watch your friends leave you behind. If she was honest, it wasn't just the fact that Sarah Tuppet had gone that made her sad, but the fact that Sarah Tuppet had gone to such a wonderful place.

Sarah had brought in photographs of her new house to show 6Y before she'd left. She'd stood proudly at the front of the class, pointing out the conservatory and the library and the treehouse, wrapped around an oak tree that looked as though it had existed since the start of time. The new house was hemmed in by woods and a stream and a stone ruin that might once have been a castle.

It was the kind of place that children in old-fashioned stories were sent to, before embarking on magical adventures featuring mythical creatures. It was the kind of place where you might find anything at the bottom of the garden.

All Emma had ever found at the bottom of her garden was a half-eaten kebab someone had thrown over the fence.

When Sarah Tuppet disappeared, she and Oleg were left at their same old school, with their same old crumbling roads, and their same old handful of run-down shops. She couldn't help looking at her house differently after that; her tiny, box house, squeezed between two others, with only a rectangle of concrete and a run-down shed for a garden. She felt guilty – she knew how hard her mum worked to keep the

roof over their heads – but she couldn't help wishing it was a slightly nicer roof.

Emma yelped as a piece of gravel lodged itself in her hand.

First, she found a crisp packet, followed by a rubber band, then an old plastic bag, and three paperclips, clipped together in a chain.

Eventually, she came across two perfectly round, black pebbles

'Are these your eyes?' she asked, holding them out towards the snowman.

'I believe so,' said the snowman. 'Because I'm currently seeing the insides of a grubby pair of hands.'

Emma passed over the pebbles and self-consciously wiped her palms on her coat. Who was the snowman calling grubby? She had showered that morning, very thoroughly, with soap that smelled of mint and lavender. It wasn't her fault that they'd ended up scampering up roofs and eating fistfuls of sugar.

'Here,' said the snowman, proffering an eye. 'You take one. It's only fair. You found them, after all.'

Emma smiled and felt her anger fade away. 'I can't take one,' she said. 'They're your eyes.'

'What do I need two for?' The snowman pushed one of

the pebbles into the middle of its face. 'See? I can see the whole world.'

Not wanting to be rude, Emma accepted the snowman's eye. 'Can I ask you something?' she said.

'All right, but quick.'

'How did you come to life? Is it because of Christmas?'

'What's Christmas?' asked the snowman.

'You really don't know?'

The snowman shrugged.

Emma thought. *How could you describe Christmas?* There were a thousand things that made it what it was, from turkey sandwiches, to cracker jokes, to writing lists and watching old cartoons and trying your hardest to fall asleep quickly so that it would come faster.

'Well,' she said, 'it's when Baby Jesus was born and the shepherds brought him stuff and your parents are supposed to bring you stuff too.'

'What's a Baby Jesus?' asked the snowman.

Emma sighed. 'Don't worry,' she said. 'I guess you know as much as we do.'

'Nope,' said the snowman. 'I know, for example, that you shouldn't be waiting around here. No, no, no. Not unless you want to be taken to the bad place.'

'What place?'

'You'll know it when you know it. But I'd leave, I would, if I were you. I'll be off after the others now. We're not dumb enough to sit around waiting to be caught.'

'The other snowmen?'

The snowman snorted. 'Have you lost your eyes as well? We're snow*women*, I should think that was quite obvious.'

Emma blushed with embarrassment and watched the snowwoman bounce away. 'Wait!' she called, wanting to ask more about the bad place. But the snowwoman didn't turn around.

Emma climbed back up the drainpipe, shook the snow out of her hair, and got back into the tent, fitting herself between Oleg and Sebastian in search of some warmth.

As she drifted back to sleep, Emma felt the snowwoman's eye in her pocket. She thought about her mum. She wondered what it would be like if she could have one of her mum's eyes and her mum could have one of hers. That way neither of them would ever be alone. Whenever they saw something beautiful or funny or scary, the other person would see it too. Even when her mum was trapped at work, she would get to see all of the weird things that seemed to be happening to Emma lately.

Emma hated Work. She imagined it as a huge, tentacled, scaly beast that sucked the life out of people. Work only ever left her mum with just enough energy to sink into the sofa and fall asleep still in her uniform. Work, Emma had decided, was not something that she was ever going to do. Instead, she would travel the world, never live the same day twice, and record her adventures in beautiful, heavy books that kids read by torchlight under their blankets.

19

'Where are we!'

'Calm down.'

'Who's that?'

'It's Emma, you idiot.'

'Not you, that thing there.'

'That's Sebastian Cole, remember?'

'What's happening?'

'Nothing's happening, just calm down.'

'It's so cold. Where are we?'

'We're on the roof of the school.'

'What?'

'In a tent.'

'Oh. I sort of remember now. I thought it was a dream.'

'It wasn't a dream.'

Oleg and Emma crawled out of their sleeping bags and sat up. It was freezing in the tent. The canvas walls hadn't managed to keep even a smidge of their body heat inside. Emma unzipped the front flap and they dragged themselves out into the morning.

'We slept at school,' Oleg said, like he couldn't believe it.

'No,' said Emma. 'We slept *on* school.'

They yawned and scrubbed the sleep crumbs out of their eyes then sat with their backs against the rattling generators.

The town was already awake. Postmen were posting post and paper boys were posting papers. Buses and cars loaded and unloaded kids. Prams were being pushed, dogs were being followed.

In the bright light of the morning, Oleg felt like he was back in the real world. There were no crows in strange vans and no unexpected goats and no cardboard spaceships. It reminded him of a night a few weeks before, when he'd woken up from a bad dream and felt like his room was crammed with monsters. Vicious things leered from the walls; beasts with many teeth crept along the carpet.

He'd tried to keep calm but eventually a yell had escaped his mouth and his dad had come hurrying in. Once he'd flicked on the light, every single one of the monsters vanished. He'd been imagining them in the darkness. 'Bad dream?' his dad had said. 'I can understand that, pal.' And then he'd climbed into bed next to Oleg and they'd fallen asleep together. It had almost been worth the nightmare to have his dad come in and speak softly to him like that.

Oleg shook his head and breathed in the snowy morning.

'Ol,' said Emma. 'Do you believe in snowmen?'

'What do you mean?'

'Like snowmen that can walk and talk.'

'Snowmen don't talk.'

'And boys don't appear in cardboard spaceships. But something's happening.'

'I'm sure there's some explanation behind Sebastian,' said Oleg. 'He probably got hit on the head and got lost and now some people from a hospital are trying to find him.'

'And he has a magic bag?'

'Maybe it's just deep.'

'And a woman in a crow mask dragged you into a van?'

'Maybe that didn't happen. Maybe I was just daydreaming or I saw it on the TV and thought it had happened to me.'

'You were terrified!'

'I'm always terrified.'

Emma snorted. 'So you think we invented someone and then someone with the exact same name and memories happened to appear in our den?'

Oleg shrugged. 'The groundskeeper said that if one

unlikely thing happens, then it's more likely that more unlikely things will happen after it. That doesn't mean impossible things are going to happen.'

'I saw a snowman,' said Emma, folding her arms in annoyance.

'Me too,' said Oleg. 'There was one outside Callie's house but she didn't have any carrots so they used a chopstick as the nose.'

'No, I saw one that talked and moved and was running to catch up with her friends. She gave me her eye and told me that we had to go, or else we'd be caught and taken to a bad place.'

Oleg rolled his eyes. 'That didn't happen.'

'But it did.'

'Didn't.'

'Did.'

'Didn't.'

'I can prove it.' She held out her palm with the black stone balanced on it. 'There,' she said. 'That's the snowwoman's eye.'

'That's a rock,' said Oleg, unimpressed.

'And also an eye,' said Emma.

'Good morning, friends!' said Sebastian Cole, emerging from the tent with a smile across his face. He stretched in the sunlight then took a seat, wiggling himself in between Emma and Oleg. 'How did you both sleep? Didn't you have the most wonderful dreams? I dreamed I was ruling over a kingdom where instead of money they used Hobnobs. Don't eat the Hobnobs! I kept telling them. They're money! Well, they went ahead and ate all the Hobnobs anyway.'

He didn't notice that neither Emma nor Oleg were responding. Instead, both of them sat staring sulkily at their hands. Oleg was ready for normal life to start again. He had barely slept, his head hurt, and his stomach felt like it was filled with excitable hamsters.

'What are we going to do now?' asked Sebastian Cole. 'I think we should find a boat and get on it. Who else?' He looked between Oleg and Emma, who were both refusing to meet each other's eyes. 'Everyone who thinks we should captain a ship raise their hands.' Sebastian Cole raised his hand. Sadly, he lowered it again.

'We have to go to lessons,' said Oleg. 'We're supposed to be getting ready for SATs.'

'What are SATs?'

'They're tests, to show how smart we are, so they can decide what happens to us when we move to secondary school.'

'To show how smart you are at what?'

Oleg wasn't sure how to answer that. 'I don't know,' he said. 'Normal stuff. Maths and English.'

'Not trout tickling?'

'You don't have to be smart to be good at trout tickling,' said Oleg.

'Right,' said Sebastian. 'If you're good at maths you're smart, if you're good at trout tickling you're just good at trout tickling.' He stood and raised one hand to his eyebrows as though he were a captain surveying the ocean. 'I don't think that's very fair to people who were born good at trout tickling,' he said.

'It's just how it is,' grumbled Emma.

Sebastian sat back down. 'So you really don't get to stay in this place for ever?'

'No,' explained Oleg. 'We'll go to secondary school in September. Then we'll be the smallest instead of the biggest.'

'And people will give us wedgies and steal our best pens,' said Emma.

'Won't the guards help you?'

'What guards?'

'The ones who walk around holding mugs.'

'They're teachers, not guards.'

Sebastian beamed. 'I like them.'

'You like everything.'

'Some of them are fine,' said Emma. 'But some of them just became teachers so they'd have an excuse to shout at children. The only person who doesn't wish we were invisible is the librarian. She gives you biscuits and will order books from Germany if you ask.'

'Will you go to the same place?' asked Sebastian. 'After they check how smart you are.'

Neither Oleg nor Emma said anything in response to that. It was a topic they had avoided like a spider. They wouldn't know for weeks whether they would go to the same secondary school, and the thought of starting all over again, in a new place where you knew no one, made them both feel sick.

They both knew that Emma's mum wanted her to take the test for St Mary's, an all-girls' school. If she got in they'd be split up for certain.

The bell rang.

'We should go to lessons,' said Oleg.

'We shouldn't!' protested Emma. 'We have to leave, right now, before that crow comes to take Sebastian away.'

'No one's coming,' said Oleg, who had managed to convince himself completely that there had been no crow-mask-wearing lady. 'And we're going to get in trouble if we stay up here.'

'We're going to get in more trouble if we wait around for whoever was in that van. We need to escape and get Sebastian away from here.'

'You always tell me not to worry,' said Oleg. 'And now I'm not worrying, because there isn't anything to worry about.'

'But there is!'

'There isn't, and we're going to be late.'

The confused boy with the magic bag looked between them, scratched his head, and followed Oleg down the hatch in the roof. Emma ground her knuckles into her forehead before following them.

✷

Mr Clay, when he appeared in the classroom, was in a better mood than the previous day. He was clutching their medieval life tests to his chest and humming. Once he'd had a look behind his desk, his mood sank.

'No register, again,' he said, shaking his head. 'I specifically went and got a new one yesterday afternoon. Did anyone take it?'

Everyone shook their heads.

Mr Clay sighed. 'I've marked your tests,' he said. 'There were a few surprises and a few disappointments, I'm afraid.

I'll hand them back now, then fetch a new register. As I promised, you all like asking me questions so much that the prize for the best test result will be one question. Whatever the question is, I will do my best to answer it honestly and fully, to the best of my ability.'

He moved around the room, handing out papers and offering comments along with them.

'Well done, Prianka,' he said.

And

'Try a little harder please next time, Kirsty.'

And

'Did you bribe an inebriated chimpanzee to sit the test in your place, Sampson?'

Sebastian Cole was given his paper last. 'Yours, Sebastian,' said Mr Cole, 'blew me away completely. Every single answer was correct, albeit rather strangely put. You have a unique way of describing things, I'll give you that.'

Sebastian beamed.

If they hadn't been so furious with one another, Oleg and Emma might have wondered how Sebastian's paper could possibly have been right when neither of them had written anything remotely sensible. Instead, they both sulked, fidgeted, and refused to look at each other.

'You are right,' said Mr Clay to Sebastian, 'that we will

never know how many died during the plague as there were no records, or "registers", being kept at the time. Some historians say it was a third of the population, some say fifty per cent, some say just ten. We'll never know for certain.'

Sebastian nodded wisely.

'And you were correct that the main cause of death was being born. Almost a third of children died before the age of five.

'You were also correct that the guards that were stationed in graveyards were there in case of zombies.

'Though these zombies were not zombies in the sense of being reanimated corpses, rather they were people who'd been buried without being dead. Medicine was so new at the time that many people didn't know how to judge whether someone was really dead or not. They'd give them a little whack, and if nothing happened, they'd go right ahead and bury them.

'In fact, most doctors could only try and ease pain, rather than cure it. Which didn't, of course, stop them trying. They drilled holes in skulls, stuck leeches on to eyeballs, and forced their patients to eat animal poo.'

Form 6Y groaned.

'Yes, a visit to a medieval doctor was more likely to put you in an early grave than cure you. You also answered perfectly about what a knight was. Like you said, a knight was a mounted soldier with land who fought in the service of God and the crown. Well done.' He beamed. 'Anyway, Sebastian, as you scored highest, you get to ask me one question.'

Everyone except for Oleg and Emma stared at the new boy expectantly. How would he use his power? What disgusting, secret, grown-up, or complicated question would he ask?

'Sir?' said Sebastian. 'What were your schooldays like?'

Mr Clay sat down.

He took off his glasses and rubbed the deep lines that divided his forehead into three segments.

'You don't know it yet,' he said, 'but childhood will always feel like home. The older you get, the further it'll feel like you've wandered from home. And you will always miss home, regardless of how difficult it once seemed.'

Sebastian Cole raised his hand. 'Sir?' he said. 'That wasn't really what I asked.'

'No,' said Mr Clay. 'I don't suppose it was. But I fear you might never listen to me again if I'm honest about my time in school.'

'We will,' said Imran.

'We don't have a choice,' said Scott Ballantine, kicking a

ball of paper at the ceiling.

'In that case, I'll tell you. But you mustn't use it against me.'

He stood up then sat back down. It was clear he was nervous. After daubing sweat off his eyebrows with a handkerchief, Mr Clay started his story.

'I was never popular in school,' he said. 'I was smaller than everyone else, my voice was squeaky, and I was desperately interested in learning. I wanted to know what the stars were called and which animals were cold-blooded and who first discovered that eggs mixed with milk and flour made pancakes.

'Most breaktimes or lunchtimes, I'd spend in the library, with books. Even if other kids didn't want to spend time with me, the characters in books didn't have a choice.' He laughed when he said that but everyone in 6Y could tell it was making him sad.

'You don't have to tell us if you don't want to, sir,' said Rachel Kiley.

'It's okay, thank you, Rachel. Now, I wanted friends very badly and I did everything to try and get them. I learned football facts and tried to share them with people, I put gel in my hair, I forced myself not to answer questions in class. None of it worked. Whenever I tried to get involved with other kids, they'd laugh and brush me off. Once or twice they'd string me along for the fun of it, but it would always turn out to be some sort of practical joke in the end.

'Then a new boy joined school. His name was Roger. He liked the same things as me and soon we were inseparable. Most days we'd go back to each other's houses to watch *Star Wars*, eat biscuits, and play Dungeons and Dragons.'

'What's Dungeons and Dragons?' asked Scott Ballantine.

'It's a game, Scott.'

'Like FIFA?'

'No, a board game.'

'Is it called that because you get bored playing it?'

Scott Ballantine high-fived Callie Jones.

'Very funny. In fact you're missing out on a world of enjoyment by not playing physical games. They engender a sense of community and fun that I fear the virtual world is sorely lacking.' He cleared his throat. 'So we got along, but I knew Roger wasn't what you'd call "cool" and I wasn't cool for spending so much time with him. It was a ridiculous thought, but ridiculous thoughts are both the best and worst thing about children. They can lead you to create marvellous things but also to treat other people in inexplicable ways.

'One morning, some of the kids who played rugby cornered me. These were the cool kids, the big kids, the kids

I'd always wanted to join in with. They asked if I knew "that freak, Roger", and I told them I hung out with him sometimes but we weren't really friends.

'"He's so weird," they said. "He must do weird stuff all the time. Tell us what weird stuff he does."

'The first thing I told them was that Roger slept with a great big cuddly rabbit called Miss Beefytoes. It seemed harmless enough. Kids would make up stuff like that about each other all the time and no one took it seriously.'

Everyone in 6Y laughed.

'But it didn't stop there. The next time they came to me, they wanted to know something else about Roger. They didn't give me much time and I panicked. I was thinking that if I gave them something good, they'd want to be my friends and I wouldn't have to hang out with Roger any more. The thing was, I loved hanging out with Roger, I just felt embarrassed for doing it. So I told them Roger had fifteen toes. He spent the next few days being chased down corridors and having his shoes pulled off his feet. Seeing ten toes never convinced them that it hadn't been a lie, they just thought he must have had an operation to get them removed.'

No one laughed that time.

'The last rumour I told them was that Roger wanted to be a teacher so much that he'd sneak into their offices and put on whatever clothes they'd left lying around. Even underwear.

'It was a horrible thing to say and I knew as soon as I'd said it that I shouldn't have. It wasn't long before the rumours were everywhere. Roger couldn't even walk down the corridor without other children shouting at him.

'The teachers thought he was strange once they'd caught wind of the rumour, even after learning that it wasn't true. Once something is stuck in your head, there's no amount of logic that'll get it out. It got so bad that Roger eventually left the school.'

'But none of the rumours were true!' shouted Imran.

'What matters isn't what's true,' said Mr Clay, morosely. 'What matters is what everyone agrees to believe.'

The children stared at him, not sure whether they were supposed to be sympathetic or horrified. It was clear he was sorry but he'd done a terrible thing too.

'Was that the end of the story?' Elissa Goober asked.

'It was,' said Mr Clay. 'Don't worry about any other tests, let's watch videos this afternoon.'

The bell rang after forty-five minutes of a white-haired man explaining atoms through the dusty TV screen.

Quietly, they all left the room.

20

The three children headed for the roof in silence. When Oleg's phone started ringing, he told them to go up without him, and he answered the call in a dark cupboard cramped with broken violins.

'Hello?' he said.

'Oleg,' said his dad. 'It's your dad.'

'I know, Dad, I can see your name on my phone.'

'Where are you?'

'I'm at school. Where else am I supposed to be?'

'Oh,' said his dad. 'What day is it?'

Oleg's dad often lost track of the days; that happened when you spent all of your time sleeping and hardly any of it looking at a clock.

'It's Friday,' said Oleg.

'Oh,' his dad said again. 'I'm sorry for shouting at you this morning.'

'That was yesterday morning,' replied Oleg, frustrated.

'Well I'm sorry, anyway. You know I'm grumpy straight after I've been woken up. I need at least a few cups of coffee to get my head straight.'

Oleg felt a surge of weary anger. 'I didn't do anything wrong,' he said. 'Don't say it like I did something wrong.'

'I know you didn't do anything wrong,' said his dad.

'Good.'

There was a long pause.

'Sometimes,' said Oleg's dad, 'I feel like I'm trapped in one of your nan's stories.'

'What do you mean?'

'She makes up all those characters but then she doesn't know what to do with them, so they get left standing around without anything to do. I'm like one of them, floating halfway through a story.'

Oleg didn't say anything. *Parents aren't supposed to tell you their problems,* he thought. *They're supposed to store them up and tell them to each other once you've gone to bed.* He didn't want to worry about his dad feeling lost, especially not when he was so busy being angry at Emma. Why couldn't she be more reasonable? Why did she always have to believe in stupid things? And why would she want to take the test for St Mary's?

'Oleg, are you okay?'

'Don't worry about me,' said Oleg. 'Worry about yourself.'

He hung up, feeling bad for his dad, but not as bad as he felt about his fight with Emma. He was tired and overwhelmed and ready to get back into his own bed and stay there.

As Oleg hauled himself up on to the roof, Emma put out a hand to slow him down.

'Don't panic,' said Emma, solemnly.

Grumpily, Oleg shrugged off her hand. 'Why would I panic?' he muttered.

'Because of that.'

She pointed over the edge of the roof at the streets below them.

21

The streets were packed with shimmering vans. On every corner, on every bank of grass, and outside every house, stood a van that mirrored the world around it. Oleg's mouth fell open.

'There are definitely a lot of them,' said Sebastian Cole. 'Someone's awfully keen to have a word with me but they give me goosebumps, which are when your skin gets upset.'

'We've heard of goosebumps,' said Emma. 'And sometimes there are good goosebumps, like when you hear a happy song or watch a sad film.'

'Yes,' said Sebastian Cole. 'Sometimes you get good goosebumps, like from lasagne.'

'Not really from lasagne,' said Emma.

'No,' said Sebastian, shaking his head. 'Not really from lasagne.'

Oleg wasn't listening. He was staring, open-mouthed, as

his hands shook.

There was no one bothering to inspect the vans or seeming at all curious over their presence. None of the people strolling past even gave them a second glance. You'd think, thought Oleg, that giant vehicles that looked as though they'd come from the future would attract some attention, even if people tended not to see the things they didn't expect to see.

'You were right,' whispered Oleg, whose heart had sunk so low he could feel its beat in his knees. 'We should have escaped when we had the chance. They knew Sebastian was at school, so we should have got as far away as possible. I'm sorry.'

'Don't say sorry to me,' said Emma, trying her best not to gloat. 'It's Sebastian they're after.'

Oleg bowed his head and turned to their newest friend. 'Sorry, Sebastian,' he said.

Sebastian waved the apology away. 'My mum always says, "Sebastian, only say sorry if you kicked over the barrel of fermenting prune juice on purpose."'

'What?' said Oleg.

'He means he knows it was an accident,' said Emma. 'Or a stupid mistake. Now do you believe we have to do something?'

'Yes,' said Oleg. 'We need to come up with a plan.'

And they did.

✶

At breaktime, everyone Oleg and Emma could trust was invited into the den for an emergency meeting. They had decided not to give people the full story about Sebastian Cole. For starters, it would take too long. For main course, none of them would believe it anyway.

Instead, they explained that Sebastian was an orphan who was being chased by a greedy uncle. Sebastian Cole's parents, they claimed, had been extremely wealthy, and when they'd died, it had put Sebastian in line for a huge inheritance. The uncle was planning to become his guardian, wait until he could claim his money, and take it all away.

'They'll stop at nothing to get their claws on him,' snarled Emma. 'If they catch him, he'll be taken away to a big draughty tower and left there until he turns eighteen and they can steal his money. We need your help to keep them away.'

'I'll help,' said Scott Ballantine, raising his hand.

'Me too,' said Callie Jones. 'If it wasn't for Sebastian, we'd be having tests every day until Christmas.'

'I'm having nothing to do with this, but I won't tell

anyone,' said Ora, hopping up and scurrying out of the den.

'What … if … Elissa … Goober … finds … out?' asked Tom Runkle.

'Leave Elissa Goober to me,' said Emma.

Everyone knew that if anyone could keep back Elissa, Emma could.

'So what do we do?' asked Rachel Kiley.

'We have to keep them out until we have a safe place for Sebastian to stay. If we manage to hold them off until nightfall, we can slip him away in the darkness. There's no way they'll be able to watch every possible exit in the pitch dark.'

'How are we going to defend an entire school?' said Scott Ballantine. 'We're not even allowed to speak during lessons.'

Elissa Goober burst in, thrusting branches aside. She was red-faced and panting.

'What's going on?' she wanted to know. 'And why wasn't I invited?'

'It's nothing,' said Oleg.

'It's private,' said Emma.

'It's an emergency,' explained Sebastian Cole. 'I am being hunted down by my sinister uncle and he has fearsome cronies stationed all around the school. We're positively surrounded! How I'll ever escape is anyone's guess.'

Oleg groaned.

Elissa Goober dug her hands into her hips and stuck out her chin as though she were about to fight anyone who questioned her. 'Let's tell a teacher,' she said to Sebastian. 'They can't let some random man take you away.'

'They have to follow the law,' said Emma. 'The uncle is his legal guardian. There's no way they're going to believe a story about a giant inheritance and a dark tower. We just need a way of distracting them until we can get him off school grounds safely.'

Elissa Goober rolled up her sleeves and took her phone out of her pocket. 'Right,' she said. 'I'm thinking he's something to do with those disco-ball vans parked everywhere?'

Oleg nodded. 'I didn't think you could see them.'

'Of course I can see them, I've not been staring into the sun. There are twenty-five out the front and another thirty stationed behind the bushes that run behind the field. No one's got in or out of any of them yet, as far as I can tell. If Sebastian's who they're after, they must be waiting for a glimpse of him before they swoop in. We'll need multiple lines of defence if we have any chance of holding them off.'

Everyone was staring at her in amazement.

'You want to help?' asked Callie Jones.

'Of course I do,' she said. 'Sebastian helped me with that stupid rat, now I'm going to help him with whatever's happening. I'm not a terrible person.'

No one said anything.

She drew a line in the dirt, with a narrow box on one side of it and a wider box on the other side. 'School's that line,' she said. 'The big box is the field and the other one's the car park. We'll need a first line of defence right at the gates, followed by a second line of defence for whoever slips past that. Third line of defence will have to be around the back, to stop them getting across the field. Got it?'

Everyone nodded.

'Who can throw?'

Several hands went up and she counted them. 'You'll need to build up piles of snowballs and wait with them at either side of the car park entrance.'

The faces below the hands nodded.

'Now, who looks oldest?'

Everyone pointed at Samuel, who was twice the height of anyone else and already had a few wisps of hair curling out of his top lip.

He bowed grandly. 'Mam says I don't look a day under forty,' he declared.

'Fine, but we'll need to get you something else to wear.

Who has a laser pen?'

Six people raised their hands.

'Okay, make sure they have batteries. Oleg, Emma, you'll need to get a suit and tie for Samuel then figure out how to defend the field. I can take care of everything out front but you'll need to deal with the back, okay?'

Both of them agreed, relieved that at least Elissa Goober had a plan, even if she wasn't yet letting them know what it was.

She had always been bossy and now Emma realised why: she was very good at being bossy, and sometimes being bossy came in very useful. Actually, bossy was exactly what a leader needed to be – it was just a word that seemed designed to stop girls taking charge.

'What about the teachers?' asked Emma. 'They're not going to let us wander around gathering supplies and crawling up to the roof.'

'Don't worry about the teachers,' said Elissa Goober. 'Leave the teachers to me.'

They stared at her.

'Get a move on,' she said. 'It's maths next.'

Mr Morecombe was in a typically grumpy mood. He did not

want to look at the children, let alone explain things to them. As usual, he dished out worksheets and told everyone to get on with them in silence.

6Y's usual tactic of irrelevant questions never worked in maths.

If you asked Mr Morecombe something off-topic, he'd simply raise his voice until you could hear your heart in your head. He was an old-fashioned shouter. It was the only way he knew of keeping control.

'What is it, Goober?' he asked, noting Elissa's raised hand.

'I need the toilet, sir.'

'Why didn't you go before the lesson?'

'I did, sir. Now I need to go again.'

Mr Morecombe sucked his teeth in disbelief. 'What on earth have you been drinking?'

Elissa Goober looked confused. 'Water,' she said. 'And orange juice and cola and blackcurrant squash and a bit of pickle juice and a strawberry milkshake.'

'Fine, fine,' said Mr Morecombe. 'Go. But be quick about it.'

Elissa Goober scuttled out of the classroom with her rucksack over her shoulder and a mischievous grin between her ears.

'What's she going to do?' whispered Oleg.

'No idea,' whispered back Emma.

'What are you whispering about?' said Sebastian Cole, rather loudly.

'Cole!' shouted Mr Morecombe. 'What is so important it needs to be discussed during my lesson? Have you finished your worksheet?'

As it happened, Sebastian Cole had finished his worksheet. It had taken him all of three minutes. This did nothing to fluster Mr Morecombe, who swiftly pulled another one out of his desk drawer and placed it on the table in front of Sebastian.

'There,' he boomed. 'Let's see you finish that one then.'

'Thank you kindly, sir,' said Sebastian Cole. 'I humbly accept your challenge.'

The next ten minutes passed very slowly for everyone apart from Sebastian Cole.

Everyone began to doubt that Elissa Goober really had a plan. How could she possibly round up every teacher? Where would she take them? It started to seem like she wasn't coming back. Maybe she'd decided to go out to the vans and tell them exactly where Sebastian was in the hope that she'd get a reward.

That was when they first heard the commotion. It sounded like a miniature tornado bowling along the corridor outside, whipping bags and coats off pegs and tearing up the carpet.

Mr Morecombe stood.

'Stay still,' he instructed. 'All of you, keep on working while I go and check what's happening.'

Nobody kept on working and nobody stayed still. As soon as Mr Morecombe headed for the door, they piled in behind him, eager to see what was going on outside.

They were not disappointed.

A trail of berries had been laid along the centre of the corridor and a goat was dashing madly along, gobbling them up. The animal had somehow managed to acquire a costume of Christmas decorations. Sparks of tinsel clung to its horns and paper snowflakes had lodged themselves in its coat.

'Ah!' bellowed Callie Jones. 'There's a cow in school!'

'That's a goat,' said Scott Ballantine. 'You idiot.'

'And it talks!'

'That was me, you double idiot.'

'I know it was, you triple idiot.'

They all watched as the goat sped past, trailing decorations, as Mr Clay, Mrs Havers, Miss Weaver, and Mr Pilling bumbled along behind it. The teachers ran like broken toys, their legs stiff and awkward. Santa hats fell from their heads and specks of glitter rained from their woolly jumpers.

'Stop the goat!' shouted Mr Clay.

And Mr Morecombe fell in behind the other teachers, chasing the blundering beast with his arms outstretched.

As it carried on down the corridor and towards the science rooms, more and more teachers were shouted out of their classrooms to join the procession that followed the goat.

Mrs Leglington joined the parade.

And Mrs Holloway-Jerkin.

Mr Dunkhowlan fell in behind her.

And Miss Hinks declared herself an expert goat-catcher before joining the back of the procession.

Soon, every teacher in school was in pursuit of the runaway animal.

The goat followed the trail of berries right into a giant cupboard. It was a cupboard where deflated balls, broken tennis rackets, and great stinking mountains of lost property were kept in precarious piles. It was a room into which no one ever dared enter. It was a room that could be smelled from four rooms away.

As the last teacher chased the goat into the dark, Elissa Goober slammed the door shut. She thrust a broom through the handles to seal it shut.

It took the teachers a good four minutes of stumbling around in the dark with a distressed goat before realising that they'd been trapped, at which point they began frantically barking threats through the solid wooden doors.

'You'll all be expelled!'

'Your parents will be called into school!'

'You'll not get any presents!'

'PlayStations will be smashed!'

'Phones will be thrown into oceans!'

'Ignore them,' said Scott Ballantine. 'When was the last

time you saw an ocean?'

Someone called for a huddle and they all put their heads in and their arms across each other's backs.

'Right,' said Elissa Goober. 'Now we need to make sure no one else can get in our way. Everyone, take a classroom. Tell them the noise they heard was someone having a tantrum. Then you need to go in, say you're a prefect and you've been sent to get something. Most of them leave the door keys in the top left drawer of their desks. Take the key, lock the door on your way out. Sorted.'

22

With the teachers shut away and every other classroom door locked from the outside, form 6Y had the entire school to themselves. It was agreed that for ten minutes they could make the most of it, then they ought to get back to the task at hand.

Knee-slide championships took place in the maths corridor.

The lunchboxes of kids with notoriously generous parents were looted.

Various unidentified powders and liquids were mixed in flasks held over Bunsen burners.

'We should stop,' said Oleg finally, as a green flame erupted from the beaker clasped between Sampson Wiley-Corer's hands.

'He's right,' said Emma. 'We don't know when they're going to start moving in. What do we do first?'

'Easy,' said Elissa Goober. 'To get the upper hand, we need to use Sebastian Cole as bait. We put him by the window in one of the classrooms facing the car park. That way, we'll know exactly where they'll be headed.'

'How thrilling!' trilled Sebastian Cole. 'I've always wanted to be bait.'

'What is bait?' asked Scott Ballantine.

'It's like a fish but smaller,' explained Rachel Kiley.

'Isn't it going to be dangerous?' said Oleg. 'What if they get to him?'

'That is why we have so many lines of defence.'

He still wasn't sure. But there was no other plan.

Everyone took their positions.

Elissa Goober was stationed on the front of the roof, where she sat cross-legged with her mobile phone in her lap, ready to text out orders.

The snowball throwers hid behind the cars of teachers.

The laser pen owners crouched behind generators on the roof.

Samuel Lugdogen rehearsed his lines in the toilet.

Nine members of 6Y headed to the canteen.

And last but not least, Sebastian Cole sat beside a window that looked out over the car park, humming happily to himself.

While everyone else was assuming their positions, Oleg and Emma were searching for a suit. They tried every office they could. In one, they found a collection of brightly coloured crystals, stashed in a wooden chest. In another, they came across a set of bagpipes.

They found a fishing rod in one office.

And a miniature pool table in another.

They looked under tiny Christmas trees, behind clay Nativity scenes, and in drawers filled with cards.

But they found no suit.

Mr Morecombe's office was their last hope.

It was the only office that was completely devoid of decorations and they entered to find it smelling pleasantly like melted cheese. Upon further inspection, the smell was coming from a portable grill that was plugged in under the desk. Golden drops of liquid Cheddar were oozing from the edges.

A small aquarium stood in one corner of the room. Fish with chameleon eyes drifted lazily around a small plastic castle.

There were posters of famous mathematicians and physicists on the walls: Neil deGrasse Tyson, Stephen

Hawking, Srinivasa Ramanujan.

They both agreed it was their favourite office so far.

'I could live here,' said Oleg.

Scrabbling through the desk drawers, they both found things that they didn't expect to find. They turned to each other. Each held up their evidence.

Oleg had found a stack of blue registers: they were all meant for 6Y.

Emma had found a driving licence: the name on it was Roger Morecombe.

Roger.

The boy from Mr Clay's past.

Both of them slumped to the floor.

They couldn't believe it.

'So,' said Oleg slowly, as though he was still trying to work it all out. 'Mr Clay bullied Mr Morecombe when they were at school together and now Mr Morecombe's trying to get Mr Clay fired by hiding his registers?'

'He probably hates working at the same place as him because it brings back bad memories.'

'But after that long, can they really still care about something like that?'

'Maybe it changed Mr Morecombe's whole life. He had to move schools. You would never stop caring if someone did something like that to you.'

'But he became a teacher, like Mr Clay said he'd wanted to be.'

'He isn't a very happy teacher. He always seems like he wants to be somewhere else.' She had a thought. 'Maybe he hates kids so much for what they did to him that he became a teacher just to get revenge on them.'

'At least he's a proper teacher; Mr Clay's only a substitute.'

'Not a good one, either.'

'But he seemed like he felt bad about Roger.'

'Feeling bad doesn't help the other person. Feeling bad just proves you knew you shouldn't have done it in the first place.'

Oleg gave her an uncertain look.

'My mum sometimes says that,' admitted Emma.

Oleg stared at the lines on his palms. Sebastian's questions had forced him to think about the future and the future looked like a scary place. 'What if when we change schools, someone says that we have fifteen toes and then people start pulling off our shoes all the time to check?'

Emma crossed her arms. 'I won't let them.'

'But what if we're at different schools? What if you get into the girls' school and I go to St Jude's and we never see each other again ever?'

'There isn't an ocean between them.'

'There might as well be.'

They shook the sad thoughts out of their heads and returned to the task at hand. The longer they searched without finding anything, the more alarmed Oleg became; and the more alarmed Oleg grew, the clumsier he became, until he was really just roving around the room knocking things over like a toddler.

'I wish we had Sebastian's bag,' said Emma under her breath. 'I'm hungry.'

'You're always hungry!' said Oleg. 'We're supposed to be coming up with a plan that stops them getting across the playing field to Sebastian and if we don't they'll take him away and we won't find him and it'll be my stupid fault for bringing him here and not believing you! If we'd gone when you said, we could have hidden, and the crows would be gone, and we could be building Sebastian his massive treehouse already.'

'Calm down,' Emma said. She felt sorry for Oleg, whose face was flushed and breathing was jagged, but she knew they didn't have time to spend being panicked.

'Sorry,' said Oleg, trying to slow his heart down.

'You okay?'

'I think so. I think I didn't want to think something was

happening because it makes me get like this.'

'I know.'

'I'm sorry I didn't believe you.'

'I know that too.'

'Did you really see a snowman?'

'A snowwoman,' said Emma. 'And yes, I really did.'

They took turns tap-tapping each other on the forehead.

A few moments later, they discovered a freshly pressed suit was waiting in the cupboard. A shimmery pink tie was thrown over the shoulder and a crisply folded handkerchief was peeking out of the breast pocket. They took one last, sad look at the pile of stolen registers on Mr Morecombe's desk and headed out to give Samuel his new suit.

✳

Elissa Goober was barking out orders. She was overseeing an operation that involved huge steel pots being overturned in front of school. The canteen had been plundered of all available foods and all such foods were being scattered across the car park. The reasoning behind this was that all canteen foods fell into one of two categories:

A. slippery foods (small, hard pellets of frozen vegetables or stale meat)

and

B. sticky foods (mulchy pastes and lumpy mashes).

The spread of foods meant that if you didn't get stuck in a sticky substance, you'd at least slip in a slippery one, and probably slide into a sticky patch.

'The food,' explained Elissa Goober, 'is just to slow them down. They'll try and swoop in all at once to make sure there isn't time for a defence. We need to catch them off guard.'

'It's bits of food, not quicksand,' pointed out Ora. 'It won't stop them for long.'

'It doesn't have to,' said Elissa Goober, scowling. 'You'll see. You two had better climb across the other side of the roof to keep watch over the field. I'll take care of this side.'

'Elissa?' said Oleg.

'What?'

'Thank you.'

'It's not for you,' she said, thumbing text instructions into her phone. 'It's for Sebastian Cole.'

23

One by one, the sliding doors of the shining vans slid open. Masked crows stepped out. Below their masks, they wore plain black shirts, gloves, combat trousers, and highly polished black boots. Some were short, some were tall, some were wide, some were narrow, and all of them stared straight ahead, eyes gleaming through the holes in their masks.

One gestured to the others and they began moving forward. They moved in perfect formation. Each crow seemed to know exactly where the others were. They would have made a wonderful dance troupe, had they been less terrifying and more interested in becoming a dance troupe.

There were audible gasps from hidden kids all around the school.

Elissa Goober sent out a group text.

Be quiet, it read. *No more gasping.*

The crows advanced steadily and surely. They walked with their arms dangling limply at their sides. As they moved, their heads bounced gently up and down as though they were fixed to their bodies by springs.

The beaks of their masks cast pointed shadows on the snowy ground.

Seeing that the tarmac was strewn with all kinds of food, the crows slowed down. They carefully stepped around old pucks of frozen hamburger and streaks of unidentifiable green sludge.

In the window of the closest classroom, Sebastian Cole fought to keep his eyes down on the book he was supposed to be reading. If they realised he knew they were coming, they'd realise it was a trap, and might get away.

Fire, texted Elissa Goober.

All of a sudden, a flurry of snowballs flew through the air, aimed straight at the heads of the crows.

They shrieked and yapped.

Skittering and scattering, they fell into each other and slipped and slid on the car park. Soon every single one of the crows was lying on a slimy mixture of damp food and half-melted snow.

Go, go, go, texted Elissa Goober.

Samuel came strutting out of the main building,

pretending to adjust his tie. The suit fitted him perfectly and his hair had been slicked back with syrup, which made him look far older but had also attracted a fly that was circling his head. No one had been able to work out how to tie the tie. Instead, they'd tied it the way you'd tie a shoelace.

'Stop where you are!' Samuel shouted in his deepest and most commanding voice. 'Go no further.'

The crows, who were mostly already stopped on account of the swamp of food, turned their heads to face him.

'We're looking for a student of yours,' one explained. Had Oleg been there to see what was happening, he would have recognised those electric blue eyes as belonging to the woman who had threatened him in her van. 'Or someone posing as a student. If you could kindly help us, we'll soon be out of your way.'

'You will not be leaving with any of the students in my care. I do not know where you come from or who you rep … rep …'

It was clear that Samuel was reading lines he'd been given from the back of his hand. It didn't matter. His size and terribly knotted tie were more than enough to lend him the air of a disgruntled teacher.

'I do not know who you represent,' he continued, 'but you are not welcome here. If you do not leave quietly, the police will be called. In fact, they have already been notified about the presence of strangers on school property.'

The crow who had spoken first carefully got to its feet amongst the slippery, sticky debris.

'I'm sure you are doing your job,' said the blue-eyed crow, 'but this goes far higher than you. Failure to comply will have disastrous consequences, not just for you, but for the wider world. We could have your entire school wiped off the map, believe me. This is not a game and you are not protecting anyone by denying us access.'

'You are trespassing,' Samuel boomed. 'This is school property. And we do not respond to treats!' He squinted at the back of his hand. 'To threats I mean, we don't respond to threats.'

His phone rang.

Without hesitating, Samuel scooped it out of his pocket, answered it, and pressed it to his ear.

He nodded and mumbled into the phone very seriously.

The crows turned to each other, confused.

Slowly, Samuel put away his phone.

'Armed police have arrived,' he said. 'They are heavily armed with very serious and powerful arms. As this is a school, they have been authorised to use very serious and powerful force.' He scrunched up his nose, trying to think of something else to say. 'They are very serious and powerful.'

Elissa Goober sent a group text: *Laser pens, go.*

Red dots appeared on the chests and heads of the crows.

'Don't move!' the leader instructed the crows.

They all raised their hands in the air. It was clear they were terrified. Samuel started to grin.

'Take off your masks,' he ordered.

None of them moved.

'I said take off your masks!'

'Please,' the main crow said. 'It's better for your sake if you do not know our faces. We shall leave now. You are making a grave mistake.'

And they turned, picking paths through mulch and getting back into their vans. Samuel forced himself to stay where he was, eyes staring ahead defiantly, until they'd all driven out of the immediate area.

Once he got back in the school, he was shaking so hard his teeth clicked like castanets in his mouth.

'That was so scary,' he kept whispering. 'They wouldn't take off their masks.'

'Shh,' said Callie Jones. 'It's done now. You did it.'

She raised his hands and the rest of form 6Y cheered.

Emma and Oleg had been sitting in the shadowy comfort of their den at the edge of the field. It was as they had suspected: once the crows had failed to gain entry through the car park, they turned to coming in across the field.

'Are you scared?' said Oleg.

'No,' said Emma. 'Are you?'

'No,' said Oleg, who was in fact very scared, but had decided to try and hide this from Emma in the future.

As the field was ringed by houses and the gardens attached to them, the crows had been forced to abandon their vans on the main road and move in by foot, through a narrow gap between two fences. They filed on to the field and spread out.

They carried black plastic devices in their hands. Oleg shuddered, thinking about what those devices might do. *Stick to the plan*, he told himself. *They'll be gone soon.*

A crackling hum seemed to be accompanying the intruders. It reminded Oleg of the wires that carried electricity past the motorway bridge. He felt his fingers tingle.

Oleg and Emma were sitting between a giant speaker they'd borrowed from the music room. It was usually used for big recitals held in the main hall. As a result, it was immensely, painfully, powerful.

Suddenly, a flash blinded the both of them.

'What was that?'

'I don't know,' said Emma. 'Just the sun.'

'My eyes hurt.'

'Quick. They're almost at us.'

Their plan was very simple.

They would cause a racket.

Both Emma and Oleg stuffed nuggets of wadded-up tissue paper into their ears. They took turns double-tapping each other on the forehead, just in case the plan didn't work and this really was goodbye.

'Go on,' said Emma.

Oleg pressed play.

The music blared from their den. It shook the leaves of nearby trees. Both Oleg and Emma could feel it reverberating through the ground underneath them. A heavy electronic drumbeat pulsed through their bones.

Almost straight away, a face loomed over a nearby fence. It was the face of a furious neighbour.

'What's that bleeding noise?' shouted the neighbour, grinding his teeth. 'Turn it down before I come over there myself and smash whatever's making it.'

With the tissue in their ears, Oleg and Emma were spared most of the threats.

The closer the crows got, the louder they turned up the music.

The louder the music got, the more furious faces appeared at the tops of fences.

'Switch that off this second!' demanded one.

'This is outrageous!'

'How dare they!'

'Who do they think they are!'

'Turn that off this instant!'

'Are we not people? Do we not have rights?'

Then, the mood shifted.

'Who on earth are they?' asked a neighbour, finally noticing the advancing troop of crows rather than just the bone rattling music. 'What are they doing on that field? They're not children from the school.'

'They're strangers!' screamed Oleg.

'Dangerous strangers!' screamed Emma.

The neighbours were horrified.

'Dangerous strangers in the school? That's not allowed.'

'Not in my backyard!'

'Someone call the police! Don't let them get away!'

Neighbours began clambering over their own garden fences and into the field. They wore bobble hats and knotted scarves. They carried tools from their gardens with them:

rakes and spades and trowels and trugs. The hodgepodge army of gardeners bared their teeth and kicked at the dirt like bulls ready to charge.

The crows hesitated.

'Get them!' ordered one neighbour.

And they all raised their gardening implements to the sky and ran as fast as any of them had run before, bounding through the snow like predators.

The crows fell to pushing each other as they all struggled to fit back through the narrow alley. They shoved each other frantically until they were free. Silently, they fled into the streets.

✱

Once the masked invaders had been chased off the field, Oleg and Emma turned back to see that the rest of 6Y had congregated on the wheelchair ramp to watch them fend off the crows.

Seeing that they'd won, everyone cheered.

Hugs and handshakes were exchanged.

Relieved sighs were sighed.

They all ran back inside to fetch Sebastian Cole and tell him the good news.

But Sebastian Cole was gone.

24

All that was left of him was his bag, lying like a sleeping cat on the chair he'd been sitting in. 6Y quickly realised they'd been fooled. The advance from the front and the advance from the back had both been distractions. While they'd been occupied with complicated plans, the crows had been sneaking into the school some other way.

How could no one have kept an eye on Sebastian? There wasn't a single member of 6Y who wasn't blaming themselves, and not a single member of the class was blaming themselves more than Oleg. How could he not have listened to his best friend? How could he not have helped Sebastian get away when they had the chance?

Everyone raced up to the roof, climbing over each other to get up the piano and through the ceiling. Once they were there, they could look out over the entire town, and they could see that all of the vans were gone. They couldn't even hear the fading sound of motors. There was no sign that the vans had ever been there.

From below, they could hear the frantic stomping of the trapped teachers.

'He's gone,' said Emma.

'I'm sure his uncle can't be that bad,' said Scott Ballantine.

'There never was an uncle!' exclaimed Oleg. 'Didn't you see those people! He's been captured by some secret organisation that wants to make him disappear because he never should have appeared in the first place. Now he's alone and probably scared and it's all my fault. They're going to make him be forgotten and he'll never get to taste cheese or tickle fish again.'

No one knew what to say to that.

Emma crouched down next to Oleg. She put a hand on each of his shoulders. 'There's no use getting angry,' she said. 'And it's not all your fault. You didn't mean to make him appear and neither did I.'

'So we just leave him now? We give up? We let them take him wherever they're taking him and just hope it's not too terrible?'

'I want to find him as much as you do, but we have to think.'

'We don't have time to think!'

'Then what do you suggest we should do?'

'I don't know,' said Oleg glumly. 'But that doesn't mean we shouldn't do anything.'

'We don't even know where they've gone.'

Scott Ballantine coughed and raised his hand. 'Um,' he said. 'I kicked one of their vans really hard.'

'That's great, Scott,' said Emma. 'But we're actually talking about something quite serious at the moment.'

Scott pulled a face. 'When I kicked it I broke that big metal thing.' He pointed down at the street. 'And now it's leaking oil everywhere, so you could probably just follow that.'

There was a pause.

Emma rushed forward to hug Scott Ballantine. 'I only kicked a van,' he said modestly.

'It's lucky you like kicking things so much.'

Scott grinned. 'I do love to kick things,' he said.

Oleg wiped a string of snot from under his nose. 'Even if we know where they've gone, how do we follow them fast enough? They're probably nine hundred miles away already.'

'That's easy,' said Emma.

★

Half a minute later, the cowboy gardener opened the door of his cabin and was confronted with the whole of form 6Y. They were all staring at him so expectantly that he took a step backwards.

'Got him, did they?' he asked, shaking his head and taking the piece of the straw out of the corner of his mouth.

Oleg nodded miserably.

'Told you they'd be coming shortly. There's too many oddities been occurring for them to let a madcap confabulation like that slip through the cracks.'

'Will you take us to them in your plough?' asked Emma, who didn't understand what the caretaker was saying and frankly didn't care. 'We have to get Sebastian back before they make him disappear.'

The caretaker took off his cowboy hat and spun it in one hand. 'I'll take you,' he said. 'But I can't be hanging around. Understand that this is dangerous for me.'

'Thank you,' said Emma.

'Don't thank me yet,' said the caretaker. He strolled around the back of his cabin and re-emerged a few seconds later, riding atop his roaring snowplough, with a straw-padded trailer fixed to the back of it.

Emma and Oleg said goodbye to their classmates.

'Thanks for trying to help,' said Emma. 'We were so close.'

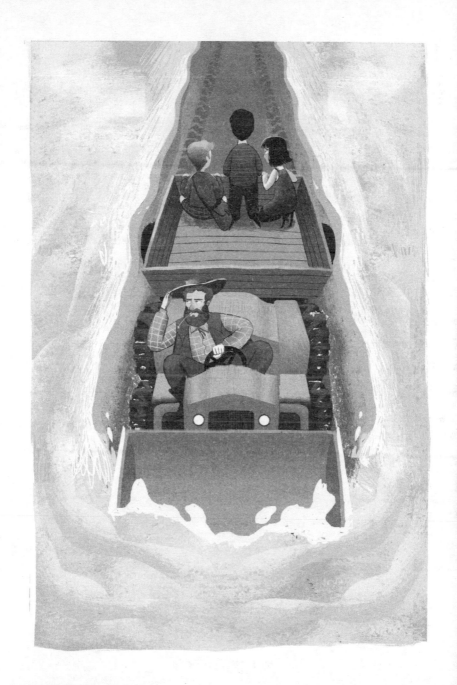

'I like Sebastian,' said Callie Jones. 'He's nice.'

'Me too,' said Ryan. 'He's funny. I hope you find him.'

'I hope we find him too.'

Elissa Goober held out Sebastian's unpredictable bag. 'Make sure you take this with you,' she said. 'I'm sure he'll want it back.'

'Thanks, Elissa,' said Emma.

'Whatever,' said Elissa Goober.

They bundled into the trailer fixed to the plough.

As the cowboy pulled out of the car park, Oleg and Emma waved to form 6Y, who had climbed back up through the music room and were waving back from the roof of the school.

25

They followed the trail of oil on the main road out of town, past the big roundabout and on to the dual carriageway. New housing estates gave way to lonely cottages, which gave way to fields, which rose into great forests, only to fall away again into snow-covered meadows studded with sheep and cows.

All the time, the sun was sinking and colour was falling out of the sky as stars popped into existence. Cars flicked on their headlights, lampposts stuttered awake.

Oleg wondered whether the trapped teachers had been released and how the rest of 6Y were explaining what had happened. Was there any excuse that might work? He guessed not.

Emma wondered whether her mum would realise she was gone. She told herself to remember to leave another voicemail once they stopped somewhere.

At a motorway service station, the cowboy pulled in and everyone used the toilets.

They shared a pot of tea in the café.

'This'll be the last stop for a while,' said the cowboy. 'Go to the toilet again, even if you don't need it. We're not stopping again unless it's absolutely necessary.'

'Do you know where the oil leads?' asked Emma. 'Do you know where we're going?' She realised that neither of them had bothered asking yet. It didn't make much difference: they were going wherever they were going and it would take as long as it took.

The cowboy exhaled loudly. 'It doesn't have a name,' he said. 'Or if it does, I don't know it. All I know is it's a terrible place. The closer we get to it, the more I can feel it tugging. It's a black hole, that place. If you listen, you can hear it.'

Neither Oleg nor Emma was convinced, but they weren't about to ask to be taken back.

Oleg sipped his tea. It was too watery. 'Who are you really?' he asked.

'That's a story for another time. Now is the time for final toilet breaks.'

In the toilets, Emma and Oleg both left voicemails for their parents. Neither expected a response. They were more of a precautionary measure.

Emma's went like this: 'Hi, Mum, I'm staying at Oleg's again, so don't worry. We're working on a project about how the Romans built roads. Don't work too hard! And make sure Oliver cleans up the kitchen.'

Oleg's went like this: 'Dad, if you listen to this, I'm fine.'

They finished up and got back on the road.

The motorway had transformed into two rivers of light: one red and one white. Lorries hauled hidden cargoes. Cars roared through the night, heading for mysterious destinations.

Where do they all have to go? Emma wondered. *Especially at this time of night.*

She turned to ask Oleg and found he'd fallen asleep, snuggled in the blanket that the cowboy had given them. She sighed. She couldn't blame him – it had been a long few days, and there was something relaxing about the rumbling of the trailer.

'Still awake?' said the cowboy, without looking back.

'Yes,' said Emma.

'I'm afraid it's probably not as comfy as your bed at home.'

'It's fine,' she said. 'What about your home? Do you miss it?'

'I miss my grandma,' said the cowboy. 'Her cooking mostly.

She used to cook a good bean stew. Black pudding, pork fat, chunks of red pepper and hot chillies.'

'Yum,' said Emma.

'It's not to everyone's taste.'

'Where is your home?'

'Home was a place you can only read in books. One book, to be precise. And not a great one. Far colder than it is here, far darker, and far more dangerous.'

Had someone made him up too? Emma wondered. *Had he escaped from a book like those green twins Oleg had been muttering about before?* It gave Emma an idea. But the idea would have to wait.

'Oh well,' said the cowboy.

'What's wrong?'

The snowplough came to a stop.

'We've run out of petrol.'

'Can't we buy more?'

The cowboy turned around in his seat. 'I don't have any money,' he said. 'I never carry much money, it tends to roll out of my pockets. The last went on that tea. Do you have any?'

Emma admitted that she didn't.

They both climbed off the snowplough and pushed it to the side of the road. Seeing a young girl and an old man stranded in the bitter cold, it didn't take long for a car to stop and offer help. They hitched their vehicle to it, and it towed them to the nearest petrol station.

'We're going to have to be slightly illegal now,' said the cowboy. 'Take my seat.'

'I can't drive,' said Emma, wishing desperately that she could wake Oleg up for support but deciding that doing so might be selfish.

'Of course you can drive. Push the thing with your foot and turn the wheel part.'

'The thing?'

'I don't know what it's called. The metal thing.'

'I think it's called a pedal.'

'Whatever it is, put your foot down on it and swing the wheel back towards the road. Don't hit other cars and only press the horn if you're genuinely excited about something.'

'But I'm a child.'

'Then don't act like a baby,' said the cowboy, hopping off his seat. 'Just make sure you're ready. If we get caught here, we're never getting your friend back.'

He plucked a nozzle out of its holster and fitted it into the snowplough. Petrol chugged along the pipe and filled up the tank in great glugs.

An attendant watched them from inside the yellow glow

of the station. Emma could see rows of brightly packaged crisps and chocolate and magazines.

Her tummy grumbled.

Maybe she could have a root around in Sebastian's bag, she thought. There was bound to be something in there. Some crumpets, maybe. Or a ham and cheese sandwich with the crusts cut off.

'DRIVE!' shouted the cowboy.

He'd thrown himself into the trailer and was motioning for her to get a move on.

She pushed her foot down on the pedal and yanked the steering wheel to the right. The snowplough shot forward. Emma lifted her foot and the vehicle came to an abrupt halt.

'Keep your foot down!' said the cowboy.

She pressed down again, and kept her foot down, as the snowplough rushed to rejoin the stream of traffic. It was all Emma could do to keep it heading straight. The rushing wind pulled tears out of her eyes and her heart hammered against her ribs.

Emma looked back in time to see the panicked attendant leap out of the petrol station and flap his arms in their direction. She knew she ought to feel guilty but all she really felt was relieved.

She pulled over when they were out of danger and let the

cowboy take his seat. 'See?' he said. 'I told you, you can drive. Adults always pretend the things they do are terribly complicated and unknowable. For the most part, they're walking into rooms and pressing buttons of one sort or another.'

Throughout it all, Oleg didn't stir; he had inherited the gift of being able to sleep through storms from his dad. Just as Emma began to drift off, a faint rain started to fall. She'd had an idea, she reminded herself. She mustn't forget it. She mustn't.

26

Just as the moon was replaced by the first glow of sunlight, Oleg and Emma woke up. They were still rattling along in the trailer tied to the plough. At some point, the cowboy must have tucked them in.

For a while, they lay looking at the sky. There were dark trails between the heavy grey clouds, like scars left behind by planes plummeting towards the ground.

Neither of them had any idea where they could be.

Except for Oleg coming from Łeba, in Poland, neither of them had left the town before.

Wherever they were, the air smelled different. It was alive with wet dirt and old bark. Inexplicably, the breeze was laced with the smell of gunpowder.

A few minutes later, the cowboy pulled off on to a narrower road, which led to a narrower road, which led to an even narrower road that wound into a dim pine forest.

Morning light struggled to find a way through the canopy of leaves. It fell in strange patterns on the dirt. Shadows shifted and flickered.

The cowboy cut the engine and hopped off the snowplough, yawning and stretching. Raindrops pinballed off branches and leaves. Crickets creaked from their hiding places.

'Is this where they're keeping Sebastian?' asked Emma, looking around uncertainly.

'No,' said the cowboy. 'This is where we're eating breakfast. I can't go on much longer without padding my belly out. Besides, he'll be fine for the moment. There's time.'

The cowboy took out a portable stove, set a frying pan on top of it, and threw in slices of bacon. Oleg and Emma sat in the trailer, with their legs dangling out and the blanket spread across their laps. In the cool of the forest, their breath made clouds in the air.

As the cowboy cooked, Emma looked around her.

She realised that what she had thought were piles of snow were in fact something quite different.

'Ol!' she shrieked, tapping Oleg on the shoulder. 'Look.'

He looked.

And then he looked closer.

And then he jumped in his seat as though he'd been

shocked by a jolt of electricity.

The forest was completely crowded with snowmen, who stood motionless between the bare trees. Some consisted of two boulders of snow, some of four. Some wore long scarves, some wore wonky top hats, and pasta bow ties and buttons that were lumps of coal. They all stared unblinkingly ahead, twig arms at their sides.

'Snowmen,' said Oleg.

'Snowwomen, actually,' said Emma. 'They're not moving,' she added, disappointed.

'Well, of course they're not,' said the groundskeeper. 'They go wandering around in the sunshine then they're sure to melt. You think they want to end up as puddles?'

'But why are they here?' asked Oleg.

'They're here for the same reason we are,' he said. 'Because they're on the way to somewhere else. My best guess'd be they're headed for the Arctic. They've got their heads screwed on, snowwomen, they know they ain't going to last long here once the weather shifts.'

The cowboy put together three sandwiches and passed them out. With the food done, he boiled water for tea, and the three of them sat in a triangle, rolling hot mugs between their hands. Oleg watched the snowwomen suspiciously, as though he expected them to leap forward at any moment.

Emma was perfectly peaceful. Having a cup of something warm between her hands had always been enough to calm her down. No matter how lost or upset she was feeling, physical heat did wonders. 'Warm hands, warm heart,' her mother used to say, forcing itchy mittens over Emma's paws.

'You said your home was a book,' she said to the cowboy, once half her tea was gone.

'It was,' said the cowboy. 'Once. A long time ago. Or maybe not. It's hard to tell sometimes. The book used to be in your library, I think, though no one ever picked it up.'

'Do you remember the story?'

'Of course. It was set in a strange world, dusty and barren, endless and still. There were small, forgotten towns, with miles of desert and rocky mountains between them. It was a lawless, new country. You could never sit still, never relax.

'You took your hand off your weapon, you could be sure someone would raise theirs against you. You fell asleep with both eyes closed, and you could be sure there would be someone waiting to pounce.

'Most nights I'd sleep under the stars. I had a reputation, you see. As soon as I entered any place, the townspeople would run into their homes and barricade the doors. They truly feared for their lives when I came around. It was so exhausting. And I was meant to snarl and shout and issue all kinds of threats. Then I'd take what I could and head back out with my horse, Dumbo. Had one eye and three legs, but he could still go like there were flames under his feet.'

The cowboy lowered his head.

'I miss that horse,' he added. 'I don't mind the plough, but I sure do miss that horse.'

'But you left?' asked Oleg.

'I never wanted to shoot anyone,' the groundskeeper said, raising his hands. 'Especially not people I was being told to shoot. It's no fun being a puppet, specially not once you've glimpsed your own strings.'

Oleg wrinkled his nose. 'Then why isn't the world full of characters from stories running around? If you can just leave books whenever you want? Why aren't there Cinderellas in the supermarket?'

'It's hard to leave the known for the unknown,' the groundskeeper said. 'Even if where you are is miserable, where you aren't might be even more miserable. Most people don't want to take the risk. And it's not an everyday occurrence. There are certain … conditions that have to be met before these things take place. Least that's what I've been led to believe. To tell you the truth, I don't know a whole lot and I'm not a whole lot of bothered.'

He swirled the dregs of his tea around the bottom of his

mug. 'Sometimes,' he said, 'I wonder if I'm just a madman. Everything feels so far away now.'

Please don't be a madman, thought Oleg.

'But my mum says she remembers you,' said Emma. 'And my brother. And there's no way you could have been that old when my mum was our age. It doesn't make sense.'

The cowboy went on speaking.

'Most people are only one stroke of luck away from lives that are happier. And you never know where or when that stroke of luck will come from. Course, it could be bad luck too. There's not much that isn't luck. Being born rich or poor, tall or short, big-eared or stubby-nosed. You might meet your future wife in a McDonald's one day or you might never meet your future wife at all.'

The children stared at him.

'Are you okay?' asked Emma.

'I'm fine,' he said. 'I'm sorry. I didn't manage much sleep last night, so I might not be making an awful lot of sense. Is everyone ready? We're almost there, and you two have a long day ahead of you.'

They emptied their mugs and piled back into the snowplough.

With one last look at the frozen snowwomen, they were on their way.

Raindrops rolled off the tips of leaves.

Birds echoed from the trees.

Woodlice stirred in rotten trunks.

27

Their destination wasn't far. Once again, it meant turning off the main road and continuing down a series of increasingly narrower roads. The last of these led through a field of neon rapeseed, somehow entirely untouched by a single snowflake, which rose up a gentle hill that looked out across a wide valley.

From the top of the hill, they saw it.

The place was a sprawling compound of grey buildings, each longer and lower than the last. A towering fence encircled the entire complex and guard towers stood at its corners.

The whole thing was like its own, hideous, colourless village. Even the snow didn't seem to want to settle on any of the buildings.

The cowboy parked in a rocky outcrop that sat high above the dismal encampment. They could make out tiny people and what looked like golf carts moving between the buildings.

The front gates clanged open and shut, admitting a convoy of trucks that had entered the valley through a separate road. It was impossible to know what they were carrying and the windows were tinted to prevent anyone from seeing in.

'This is where I leave you,' said the cowboy, slapping the steering wheel between his hands.

Neither Oleg nor Emma moved from the trailer.

'You can't go,' said Oleg.

'Why not?'

'Because you need to help us.'

'This place isn't safe for me. I'm lucky I've come this far without being caught, but once you settle into the world, they find it harder to catch you.'

Oleg and Emma climbed out of the trailer.

'Good luck,' said the cowboy, tipping his hat. 'I'll ask the universe to take care of you.'

And he disappeared back over the hill.

✶

They sat in the field at the edge of the building for an hour, trying to come up with a way of gaining access to the compound. Every suggestion seemed worse than the last.

Emma suggested waiting until more trucks arrived, then climbing into the back of them, until they realised that more trucks might never arrive.

Oleg suggested disguising themselves and demanding to be let in, until they realised they had no idea who they ought to be disguising themselves as.

Finally, Emma decided to go looking for help in Sebastian's bag. She did not pull out chicken nuggets or trifle or a crisp sandwich; she pulled out what looked like a remote control. Unidentifiable pictures were stamped on the buttons. One looked like a hot dog, another resembled two smiling sheep.

She held it up to her ear and shook it. The remote control made no sound.

'What do you think it's for?' she asked.

'I don't know. Maybe it's dangerous. You should probably put it back.'

'What's the worst it could do?'

'It could explode us.'

'How would it explode us?' Emma held it out ahead of her and pressed down on the first button.

Oleg sighed. 'It obviously doesn't do anything.'

Emma was grinning. 'Yes, it does,' she said, pointing over Oleg's shoulder. He spun around to find Sebastian's spaceship standing behind him. Tracks of blue lights blinked across its body. Wisps of smoke wound out of its corners.

'Well?' said Emma.

'Well what? How is that going to help us?'

Emma raised her eyebrows, as if to remind him to believe in things a little more.

Oleg threw up his hands in defeat. 'Okay,' he said. 'Let's go in.'

Emma shuffled past on her hands and knees, pushed open the door, and squeezed herself in. Oleg heard her gasp.

'Quick,' she said. 'Come on.'

Oleg followed.

Inside, Sebastian Cole's spaceship was the size of a reasonable double bedroom. There were two reclining seats, a wall of screens showing maps and figures, a microwave, a roll-top bathtub, and a big metal panel of buttons, slides, switches, screens, and unidentifiable bumps.

There were no windows to the outside world in the spaceship. Instead, one long panel of glass revealed an endless darkness, spotted with stars.

Floating in the blackness was Planet Earth.

They both stared. Even if it wasn't really the earth, it was still a picture of every single bent spoon, library book, mum, pair of sandals, cinema, stopwatch, Labrador, and chessboard in existence. It didn't look like much. It reminded Oleg of some kind of exotic vegetable.

'See?' Emma said, pointing to the globe. 'Our schools won't be that far apart.'

Oleg took the seat next to Emma. Cautiously, he placed his arms on the armrests.

'Why is there a bathtub?' he whispered. 'What kind of spaceship is this?'

'Why are you whispering?' whispered Emma.

'I'm not sure,' whispered Oleg.

The computer console in front of them came to life.

'Welcome to the MicroAstral 9000,' said the spaceship. 'Your first choice in personal galactic travel. I am here, to get you there.'

'Um,' said Oleg. 'Hello?'

'And hello to you too, tiny sir. How may I be of service today?'

'We need to get into that place just down below. That big scary-looking place. And we don't want anyone to see or hear or notice us.'

The computer bleeped and blooped. 'It is on radar,' the spaceship said. 'Unidentified nine-unit compound, one hundred and twenty metres down. Do you have a preference for a location within the target?'

'We're not sure,' said Emma. 'Just the middle maybe?'

'Just the middle, coming up,' said the MicroAstral 9000. 'Please remain seated during the journey. Keep your hands and feet to yourself at all times. Do not hesitate to request refreshments. Kindly avoid flushing the toilet during take-off and landing. Enjoy your flight.'

The ship rocketed upward.

Oleg and Emma were thrown back in their seats. It felt like invisible hands were tugging at the skin on their faces. Emma's stomach churned and bubbled. Oleg's head pounded.

They rose.

And spun.

And rolled.

It made no sense at all as a way down to where they were going. Oleg worried that the spaceship had misunderstood and decided to take them to some distant galaxy.

When the spaceship finally came to a stop, both of the children were pale. Emma clutched her belly and Oleg had his hands over his ears.

'Can we open the door?' he asked. 'Is it safe?'

'It is safe to exit the craft,' said the spaceship. 'Thank you for choosing to fly MicroAstral, we hope to see you again in the future.'

Emma bounded out. Oleg followed behind her, walking unsteadily.

They found themselves beneath an unending sky dotted with thousands of stars, each one sharper and closer than they'd ever been. At first, they just gazed up at the ceiling. Each pinpoint of light seemed so much closer, as though the stars could be caught in your hand. But there was something not quite right about the whole thing. The stars were passing around each other and moving in arcs and circles, leaving behind glimmering trails.

'Oh my God,' said Oleg. 'We're actually in space.'

He held out his arms as though he was expecting to float.

'We're not in space,' said Emma, banging her heel on the ground. 'We're standing on floor. There's no floor in space. There's just … space.'

Embarrassed, Oleg dropped his arms. 'Then where are we?'

'You're in a planetarium,' said a voice.

The children jumped.

28

A woman stepped out of the shadows, her shoes clicking on the floor as she walked. She wore a long white lab coat, smeared with technicolour stains as though it had been worn during a paintball match. Her hair was so scruffily cut you might have guessed she'd hacked at it herself in the dark, which she had. Doodles and equations had been scrawled up her arms in marker pen. Stubby pencils were balanced behind her ears.

'The Predictionary Planetarium of the Institute of Unreality, to be exact. Designed to offer an exact model of the sky above our heads.' She winked. 'Don't worry,' she said. 'I'm not one of the baddies.'

'Then what are you?'

'A lowly scientist, who's been trapped here for the past ten years. Technically I signed a piece of paper, and technically I'm being very well paid, but there's also nothing for me to spend the money on. I could order a few new coats, I suppose, and I've always fancied those shoes with the wheels that pop out.'

As she said that, the scientist slid across the floor on her knees and examined the path of a star overhead. She narrowed her eyes and followed it with a finger.

'You've been here ten years?' asked Emma.

'Give or take,' said the woman. 'I have a bedroom, I have a toilet. Meals appear, empty plates disappear. It's not the end of the world. You're not my first hallucinations either. I get so lonely, I invent all kinds of people. Two weeks ago I had a wonderful picnic with two gorillas.'

'We're not hallucinations,' explained Emma. 'Or gorillas. We're children.'

'False dichotomy,' said the scientist. 'You could be hallucinations and children, or you could be gorilla children.'

'Well, we're not,' said Oleg.

'If you say so.'

The scientist climbed a set of stairs that shot up out of the ground each time one of her feet stepped forward. She rose higher and higher, coming closer to the stars. At the top of the dome, she reached out and drew a line with her finger from one star to a blue speck that was pulsing in the darkness.

The scientist mumbled to herself.

She leaped forward, into the open air. Oleg and Emma both held their breath. Half a second before the scientist hit the floor, a pair of robotic hands lunged out of the corners of the room and caught her under the armpits, slowly lowering her to the ground. If she noticed it happening, she did a perfect job of pretending not to.

She fell to her knees and pulled open a panel filled with flickering switches and glowing buttons. The scientist tapped, twisted, and clicked various buttons before muttering under her breath.

In a notepad, she scrawled a complicated pattern, then held it up and scrutinised it against the night sky.

'Sorry,' said Emma. 'But what exactly is this place for?'

The scientist slammed the panel shut and jumped to her feet. 'Well, my little corner is set up to predict certain alignments and configurations of planets, asteroids, comets, and suchlike. This station is particularly concerned with Asteroid B612, otherwise known as the rock of unreality, or the disruption stone, first discovered by Baron Franz Xaver von Zach in the eighteenth century.'

'But what does that have to do with Sebastian Cole?'

'You'll have to forgive me,' said the scientist, 'but I've never heard of Sebastian Cole. Is it another asteroid of some kind?'

'He's not an asteroid, he's our friend. He appeared out of nowhere and then these crows came to take him away and the cowboy said he'd be here.'

'Ah-ha,' said the scientist. 'He appeared out of nowhere?'

'Well, we sort of made him up, then he appeared, in that spaceship we just arrived in, but in our den at school.'

'Makes sense,' said the scientist.

'Does it?'

'The asteroid doesn't come around often and predicting when it will is almost impossible. When it does fall into a certain alignment, it can interfere with subatomic activity and introduce wild unpredictability into life on earth. In short, B612 has the ability to render the impossible, possible.'

'But how?'

'How did the universe ever come to exist? It doesn't particularly matter; all that matters is that it's true. For a period of time, anything can happen. Most anomalies are small and pass unnoticed: extra coins in pockets, trees growing overnight, inexplicable monsoons.

'Sometimes they're bigger, and fish fall from the sky or village idiots find themselves in charge of huge empires. It is the role of my employers to cover these events up or explain them away as best they can.'

'Why?' said Oleg. 'Why can't they just leave them alone?'

'There are any number of reasons,' said the scientist. 'The information could cause panic or fear. It could lead to people second-guessing the nature of reality. The problem,' she continued, 'is that once something impossible has a foothold on earth, more impossible things tend to follow, and things become increasingly difficult to control. I'm assuming that's why they made off with your friend.'

Without thinking, Oleg and Emma moved slightly closer together. It was all starting to make some kind of sense: the goat, the snowwomen, and the boy with the bag – one impossible thing after the other. Would there be more to come?

'Is there a way of getting him out?' asked Oleg.

'You've seen this place: watchtowers, barbed wire fences, dogs. You'll need a better plan than finding him and running out.'

'We have a spaceship.'

'So you do,' said the scientist. 'And a mighty fine vessel it is too. You'll find a door across the room. It'll take you on to the main star corridor. Follow that to the end, take a left. You'll be in a glass tunnel. Follow that to the end and turn right. I'm almost certain your friend will be in one of the rooms along there. The code for every door is 2002 – they're too lazy to change them to anything else.'

'If you know all the codes,' said Oleg, 'why don't you escape yourself?'

'Escape is not always about getting away,' said the scientist. 'Now wait here one second.'

She disappeared through a hatch in the floor then climbed back out, carrying two white coats folded over her arm. 'Wear these,' she said. 'They won't be much help if they get close, but from a distance you might get away with it.'

'Thank you,' said Emma.

'My pleasure,' said the scientist. 'I hope you find your friend. Be warned, though. Even if you manage to escape this complex, you won't be home free. This institution has a reputation for being remarkably thorough and thoroughly relentless. If your friend does not conform to the natural laws of our world, he will continue to throw it into disarray, and there will be disastrous consequences.'

Emma remembered her idea from the night before. If it worked, Sebastian wouldn't have to surrender and they'd never catch him either.

'We'll be fine,' she told the scientist.

'Perhaps,' said the scientist. 'Until the comet has passed, any number of impossible things might happen.'

29

Strip lights in the ceiling made the corridor blindingly bright after the darkness of the planetarium. Both Oleg and Emma lifted the sleeves of their white coats to cover their burning eyes until they slowly adjusted.

'You okay?' Emma asked.

'I'm okay,' said Oleg.

'We should have brought sunglasses.'

Oleg dropped a hand on to Emma's shoulder. 'Was she saying that we're going to have to get rid of Sebastian or else the world will end?'

'I think so,' said Emma. 'But I've had an idea for how we can keep him safe and stop everything from turning into a mess.'

'What is it?'

'I'll tell you if we ever get out of here.'

They dropped the coats from their eyes. Oleg picked up the

spaceship, which they'd quickly discovered weighed about as much as a pencil case, and they shuffled on.

The corridor was strangely boring and boringly beige. It could have been any corridor in any school or office. It even smelled the same: a slightly sticky mix of plasticine and stationery.

They padded to the end and took a left, just as the scientist had said.

And, just as the scientist had said, they entered a glass tunnel.

A leafy green light fell over everything in sight. Through the ceiling of the tunnel, they could see swaying trees, linked by ragged vines and rickety wooden structures.

The tunnel was muggy, as though they were walking across the floor of a rainforest. Birds squawked. Bugs droned and whistled.

Neither of them knew what to say. As they moved along, their clothes grew heavy with sweat.

It was a relief when the tunnel ended, and they found themselves back in another dull corridor painted in a combination of browns and greys. Oleg put down the spaceship and dabbed sweat off his forehead.

'That was weird,' he said.

'Weirdly hot,' said Emma.

'Should we check all the rooms?'

'I think so. You do that side, I'll take this side. Remember, the code's 2002.'

They got to work.

In his first room, Oleg found nothing but blue walls completely covered in tiny drawings of whales.

In her first, Emma came across an aquarium shaped like a wrecked ship and packed with tiny silver fish that swam in complicated patterns.

Then Oleg saw a room full of mannequins dressed up like Tudors.

And Emma found a collection of ancient Egyptian artefacts balanced on plinths.

Oleg walked in on what looked like a deserted circus tent.

Emma discovered a cricket pitch.

They took a break and Emma took over spaceship-carrying duties.

'What if he's not here?' Oleg asked. 'Maybe the scientist was wrong. Maybe the caretaker was wrong too and we're in completely the wrong place.'

'No,' said Emma.

Not wanting it to be true, she charged to the next door, keyed in the code, and flung it open.

Inside was Sebastian Cole, sitting serenely with his legs crossed. He was in a completely white room with no windows. The blankness of the space made it difficult to tell how long it went on for. It could have been a cathedral and it could have been a crypt.

Sebastian looked up and smiled when he saw his friends. He bounced to his feet.

'You came!' he exclaimed. 'I knew you would. I knew you'd never forget. They said I was a goner and I told them that I was, in fact, the very opposite. I was an un-goner. I was still here.'

'Of course we came,' said Oleg. He felt ten times lighter now that he knew their third friend was alive and well. The weight he'd been carrying since they'd found his bag lying lonely on a chair evaporated. His mistake wasn't unfixable. Sebastian Cole wasn't gone.

'We need to get moving,' said Emma, through a smile. 'Otherwise we're going to lose our third friend for a second time. That's why we've brought your ship.' She crouched and set it down on the ground. They all admired it.

'How did you find her?' asked Sebastian.

'We pressed a button on a remote control and it appeared.'

'Ah,' said Sebastian Cole. 'The megatron. A fine tool, I'm sure. Though I've never had cause to use it myself. I've often wondered what exactly it does, you know. I had suspicions that it was linked to the stars and if I started pressing things they might start falling out of the sky.' He blinked. 'Let's go, let's go. This place is deafeningly quiet. It's beginning to make me feel as though I've disappeared already.'

The three of them piled into the spaceship. Sebastian and Emma took the seats while Oleg lay in the bathtub, his legs flopped out of one side. Drawing a control towards him, Sebastian began pressing buttons and flicking switches.

'MicroAstral,' he said. 'It's Sebastian Cole here.'

And just in time.

They could hear the creak of a door being pulled open and the pounding of footsteps as crows filled the room in which the spacecraft stood. Outside the ship, the heels of heavy boots drummed the floor.

'Is it a bomb?' Emma heard one of the crows ask another. 'Where are they?'

Sebastian madly clicked at the controls as though they were a PlayStation controller.

'MicroAstral,' he said, giving the machine a gentle thump. 'MicroAstral, can you hear me?'

'I feel sick,' said the spaceship. 'I've got a poorly tummy.'

'Come on,' Sebastian whispered. 'You can do it.'

'I can't do it,' said the spaceship.

'You can!'

'I can't.'

And it buzzed, hummed, and let loose a sigh of smoke from one corner of the control panel.

'What is it?' asked Emma. 'Why isn't it going?'

'The ooberator,' said Sebastian Cole. 'I told you the ooberator tends to play up. Wretched thing. It's a miracle you got it started in the first place.'

'So what do we do?' shouted Oleg. 'How do we fix it?'

'Oh, there's no way of fixing an ooberator. Fixing an ooberator's like trying to fix a thunderstorm. Your only plan of action is to wait until it passes.'

'So the ship's useless?' asked Emma.

'Don't say that,' said Sebastian Cole, looking hurt on behalf of his ship. 'She knows any number of fascinating facts, can sew on buttons, and runs the most relaxing bath in the history of relaxing baths. You can't expect her to be ready to zip about all the time. What about—'

He was cut off by the rasping voice of one of the crows waiting outside.

'Kindly step out of the personal spaceship,' it said. 'If you do not step out, we will be forced to detonate the craft.'

'Should we go out?' asked Sebastian Cole. 'I think our options might be to go out or be dragged. I've never been a fan of dragging myself.'

'Or detonating,' said Emma. 'Nothing good ever detonates.'

One by one, they stepped out, back into the never-ending white of the room.

The beaks of the crows' masks looked down on them.

'What should we do with them?' asked one.

'Confiscate the spacecraft,' replied another. 'And lock them all in here. There's nothing to be done for now. Bring them to the general when he's back from Ballyhoo. I expect the real ones will need to be taken up north. Normal disintegration procedure remains in place for the confabulation.'

'I think that's me,' whispered Sebastian Cole.

Two of the crows lifted the ship and carried it out with them. Another two forced Oleg and Emma to turn out their pockets, then took their phones. It was no use protesting. As the last one left, the door was locked, double-locked, and triple-locked. The three of them were left alone in the plain white room.

'Oh well,' said Sebastian Cole. 'It was very kind of you to try rescuing me. Don't go thinking I'm not grateful. In fact, I'm positively over the moon.'

Emma sank to the floor and pressed her face into her knees.

Oleg closed his hands into fists and held them against his eyes.

30

They sat in the white room for hours and hours and hours and hours and hours. Without a clock and with the light never changing, none of them knew what time it was. It was impossible to tell whether only minutes were passing or entire days were slipping away. When they tried to explore the room for ways of getting out, they only stumbled on to more white space; no walls, no windows. They couldn't even find the door they'd come in through.

At first, Emma tried to keep count of the hours by making scuff marks on the white floor with her shoes. Soon enough, the scuff marks blended into one big patch of black. She hadn't been sure she was making the hours long enough anyway. Did a second last 'one Mississippi' or 'one hippopotamus'?

While Oleg and Emma sat quietly dreading whatever might come next, Sebastian bounced around the room swinging his arms.

Eventually he came to a stop and asked whether either of them wanted to play a game.

'Like what?' said Oleg, miserably. 'Hide and seek?'

'Or I-Spy?' said Emma.

'You two are so funny!' said Sebastian Cole. 'We could do anything. We could play quiz or I went shopping or tag? Once, I was trapped in a well and I invented an entire universe. There were talking horses and dragons and a city under the sea. While I waited for someone to find me, I just wandered around that universe going on quests.'

But neither of them felt like playing.

After a while, they noticed Sebastian Cole jerking weirdly about in one corner of the room. He was bending and twirling and jumping and lunging with a grin plastered across his face and his eyes sparkling.

'Um,' said Oleg. 'Sebastian?'

'Yes?' said Sebastian, turning and lowering his arms.

'What exactly are you doing?'

'I'm creating a dance,' said Sebastian Cole. 'It's a dance based on the story of how we got here. This part is the trout tickling.'

He bent down low, tickled an imaginary fish, then threw his arms up in the air.

'And this part is when they chased us in the car.'

He skipped joyfully in a circle.

'And this part is when they came to the school and you thought you'd got rid of them but they secretly got in and took me away in a van and it was truly terrifying.'

He fell to the floor and dragged himself along it as though invisible people were pulling him away.

Oleg stifled a laugh.

Emma got to her feet. 'All right,' she said. 'Teach me the dance.'

What felt like an hour later, all three of them had perfected the routine. It made no sense and bore almost no resemblance to actual dancing, but it did do something to lift their spirits. Exhausted, they dropped to the floor to catch their breath.

'You are both very talented dancers,' said Sebastian Cole.

'Is he being sarcastic?' asked Emma.

'I don't know,' said Oleg.

Sebastian Cole sat up on his elbows. 'I'm glad you wrote about me,' he said. 'I'm sorry your other friend went away.'

'That's okay,' said Emma. 'You were a good Sarah Tuppet. Even if her house has a fireplace, she probably doesn't get to do as much fun stuff as we did.'

'I liked running away from people with you,' said Sebastian.

'Me too,' said Oleg. 'I was scared but not just that. I don't think you have to not be scared. You just have to be scared and something else too.'

'Hungry?' said Emma.

'Maybe,' said Oleg.

They froze in position as the door was flung open. A single crow stood behind it, dressed entirely in black, with one of the masks tied around its head. The crow took in the smiling children, sitting in a semicircle on the floor. It appeared confused, though it was difficult to tell exactly what it was feeling.

'You will follow me now,' said the crow.

'All of us?'

'All of you. Come. Quickly.'

They traipsed out of the room. The relief that came from dancing had disappeared as soon as they'd glimpsed the curved beak of the crow's mask.

'It's okay,' Oleg whispered to himself. 'It's all okay.'

The corridor was dimmer now, lit only by tiny circular lights in the walls. It felt like being on an aeroplane at night. It felt, Oleg thought, like being on an aeroplane that was about to crash-land in a wilderness.

None of them could imagine where they might be headed. The cowboy gardener had mentioned a room where they'd be left until they were forgotten. They wouldn't be forgotten, surely? They had teachers and uncles and cousins and friends. None of them would forget.

Oleg wondered whether his dad would remember him, or whether he'd just carry on sleeping. He touched the crescent moon scar on his leg and promised himself that he'd wake up Dad if they got out of this, even if it meant upturning buckets of ice-cold water over his head or having to drag him off the sofa or pour hot coffee straight into his mouth.

Oleg put his hand in Emma's.

Emma wondered whether her mum would remember her either, when the crows tried to make them disappear, or whether she'd be too busy with work. She wondered whether work would ever end, or whether it would just go on and on, with their house growing emptier and emptier as more grisly men turned up to carry things out of it.

And who would remember Sebastian Cole?

They would. They would both remember Sebastian Cole so much that it would be impossible for him to disappear.

The crow was walking fast and the three of them struggled to keep up.

Midway along another seemingly endless corridor, they were stopped by another crow going in the opposite direction.

'Where are you taking them?' it asked suspiciously, crouching to get a better look at the children. They saw two perfectly black eyes glaring out of slits in the mask. Breath that smelled of overbaked eggs leaked out on to their faces.

'To see the general,' said the other crow.

'The general only wanted the corporeal ones,' said the new crow, straightening up. 'The confabulation is to remain in the room of forgetting.'

'The general changed his mind.'

'Are you certain?'

'Yes,' said the crow, uncertainly. 'I am certain.'

They moved to one side for the other crow to move past. For some reason, the one who had taken them waited until the questioner had gone before moving. Their crow was hopping from foot to foot as though it was nervous. Its hands danced around its hips as though they were searching for pockets that weren't there.

'Hurry,' it said, once the footsteps had faded out.

'What?' Emma asked, confused. 'Why?'

'Just hurry up! Run!'

The crow took Sebastian and Emma by the hand and Emma took Oleg by the hand and they all ran full pelt down the corridor, shoes squeaking on the old plastic floor. They weren't sure why they were holding hands with the crow or why they were suddenly in such a rush.

The crow ran on and threw itself through a door.

They barrelled along a dark passage and hurried down a set of metal stairs that led to a narrow tunnel carved out of stone.

Around one corner.

And another.

They could hear panicked, angry voices coming from somewhere up ahead.

'This way,' yelled the crow, yanking them into a cramped cupboard filled with cleaning supplies. Old mops stood in buckets of mucky water, jars of nails lined the shelves, and a white mouse peered out of a dark hole.

The crow pulled off its mask.

The crow wasn't a crow.

The crow was the scientist.

She shook loose her hair and tossed the leather mask on to a shelf.

'I realised you were real!' she explained, beaming. 'You left footprints all across the planetarium.

The imaginary gorillas never leave footprints.'

'And you came to help us?' asked Emma.

'Trust me, there's no way you're getting out without my help.'

'But why do you suddenly want to get out?'

'It's an impossible day,' said the scientist. 'What better day to try and escape? Now shush. They're about to pass us. They already know you're gone and they'll be closing everything down.'

They listened as a stampede of crows marched along the corridor.

'What now, sir?' asked one.

'Lock down the wing, from top floor to lowest basement. They must still be in here somewhere. No one is to go out or in until we have them back. Do you understand?'

'We understand.'

They split into groups and jogged off in different directions.

'What do we do now?' asked Emma. 'Wait here?'

'Or should we prepare for a long and dangerous battle?' asked Sebastian Cole.

'No,' said the scientist. 'There is to be absolutely no battle.'

'But I've always wanted to be in a battle,' said Sebastian Cole, sulkily.

'He's always wanted to be everything,' explained Oleg.

'If you want to make it out, there's only one way that's safe. None of the higher-ups even know it exists. We manage to get out that way, and it'll buy us time to get as far away from here as possible. But it means getting into the rainforest first.'

'We saw that through the tunnel,' said Emma. 'Is it a real jungle?'

'As real as you or me. It appeared in a leisure centre near Derby thirty years ago and they had it brought here for safekeeping.'

'How come you found the way out?'

'I spend a lot of long nights alone,' said the scientist. 'Sometimes, I can't sleep for days. And there's nothing much to do but explore. None of the rest of them seem to mind as long as I don't set fire to anything or free any animals.'

'We saw mummies and a fish tank shaped like a ship.'

'Yes,' the scientist said. 'Housed here is one of the largest collections of impossible things this side of the River Ribble. There is an almost endless number of strange things waiting behind the doors of this centre.'

'I still don't understand how we'll get from the forest thing out of here,' said Emma.

'You'll see,' said the scientist. 'Now come on.'

31

On the balls of their feet, they tiptoed down the dark passage. Everyone was listening for the sound of approaching crows. They could hear thuds from overhead and rustles from underneath but nothing seemed to be on their level.

'This way,' said the scientist.

They climbed a rickety ladder and crossed a bridge over an empty darkness. Emma wanted to know what was down there. Oleg wanted to forget that 'down there' existed. He walked with his eyes shut and his hands firmly grasping the shaky rope supports. In his head, he pictured his bedroom and a bowl of pistachio ice-cream. It all felt so far away.

'Are we almost there?' he asked once they'd reached the other side.

'Not really,' said the scientist.

'But no more bridges?'

'Probably not,' said the scientist. 'Now listen. We're about to get back on to the busier floors. If we get split up, try your best to make it to the forest, then head for the tallest tree.'

'Let's not get split up,' said Oleg.

'But Sebastian's always wanted to get split up,' giggled Emma.

Oleg grinned despite himself. Sebastian Cole laughed until his laughter became dangerously loud and the scientist told him to bite down on his arm. He did. He bit down until his eyes watered and all traces of anything funny evaporated.

A long, steep slope of mud led them up to a kind of washroom which the crows used to change dirty wellies for clean shoes. A door at one end led back into the maze of boring corridors.

They took the first corridor at a steady pace. Not fast enough to be heard but not slow enough to be caught. Everyone was conscious of every sound. They heard their hearts in their heads.

The scientist raised a hand to get them to stop.

Someone was coming.

She shoved them into the nearest room.

They found themselves in a stone chamber. Stalactites hung from the ceiling and stalagmites rose from the ground. Glowing pools of clear blue water held silver fish shaped like butterflies.

Sebastian Cole reached out a hand to pluck a glittering stone from the wall.

'Don't touch anything,' ordered the scientist.

He dumped his hands in his pockets.

Once they were certain the coast was clear, they headed back out. They continued down the corridor. Around the next corner, they came face to face with two crows.

The crows had been waiting for them. They were carrying long batons made out of heavy wood and leaning casually against the walls. They grinned. Clearly, they'd known where the escapees had been the entire time.

'Run!' urged the scientist.

And they did.

But the crows had longer legs than any of them.

Oleg chanced a look back.

'Ol!' shouted Emma.

He ran on.

A hand reached out and grazed his shoulder. She almost had him. He felt her fingernails catch at his clothes.

'Help!' he pleaded.

The scientist dug fingers into the corners of her mouth and blew out a piercing whistle that tore through the air like an arrow. 'Duck,' she barked to Oleg.

'Where?' shouted Oleg, terrified.

'Not a duck, just duck.'

He ducked.

And a goat came running in the opposite direction. It flew down the corridor, aiming itself directly at the crows. As Oleg closed his eyes and pressed his forehead into the floor, the goat launched itself over him and tackled the two crows to the ground.

He breathed a sigh of relief and leaped to his feet.

'Thank you,' he told the goat, who was entirely in control of the two flustered crows. It had a hoof on each of their chests. Each time one tried to get up, the goat lowered its face and growled. There was something remarkably commanding about it. It was not the kind of goat you wanted to be on the wrong side of.

In a shadowed alcove, they stopped to catch their breath.

'Where did that goat come from?' Oleg asked.

'When I said they don't like me letting the animals out,' explained the scientist, still gasping for air, 'I didn't say it stops me doing it. Nothing deserves to be cooped up in here. I know how it feels. The one they liked least was when I set free the rhino they'd found in a swimming pool in Wales. Olga, her name was. They caught her sleeping behind the fur coats in a charity shop.'

'But that goat was at our school,' said Oleg in disbelief. 'It was what Elissa Goober used to round up the teachers so we could save Sebastian.'

The scientist shook her head, smiling. 'It's what happens,' she said. 'Unlikely things breed unlikely things. It's how we got from inventing light bulbs to landing on the moon.'

Once everyone was ready to go, the scientist issued her instructions.

'We're about to reach a narrow tunnel,' she explained. 'And you're about to have to run faster than you have before. Run and run and just keep running. Don't stop for anything. If we get through there, we'll be almost in the jungle, and I know that place better than any of them ever will. Got it?'

'Got it,' said Emma.

Oleg reached up and double-tapped the scientist's head.

'What was that for?' she asked.

'Good luck,' Oleg told her.

32

The scientist ran ahead.

    With Sebastian behind her.

    Oleg behind him.

And Emma at the very back.

At the far end of the tunnel, shafts of moonlight tied a domed ceiling to the ground. They ran on. The moonlight brightened.

As Emma sped up, a door flew open behind her, and a face appeared in the doorway, half-hidden in the shadow. It was a crooked face, with a mouth full of yellowed teeth.

'Quick,' said the face. 'If you keep going that way, you'll run into a trap.'

Emma came to such a sudden halt that she almost toppled forward. 'Who are you?'

'It doesn't matter who I am, only that I'm on your side. Do you want to see the outside of this place?'

'Yes.'

'Then hurry,' urged the face, beckoning her into the shadow. 'There's no time.'

Emma called out for Oleg and Sebastian to stop. 'This way,' she shouted.

Without a second thought, they turned on their heels and barrelled after her, through the doorway.

By the time the scientist looked back, it was too late.

Oleg, Emma, and Sebastian Cole were already through the door.

And the door had clanged shut. No sooner had the three of them stepped through the doorway than ropes leaped out of a dank stone wall and bound them. It happened so suddenly that none of them had time to take it in.

They were in a towering hall built of cold, green-veined marble. Every sound echoed endlessly between the towering walls.

Standing in front of them was a man, bent in half laughing. He was dressed in a black vest covered with bulging pockets and wearing dark leather boots that came up to his knees. His cheeks hung over each side of his jaw like a dog.

'So easy,' he muttered to himself between giggles. '"You have to come this way," I said. And then they came this way. They came this way! "I'm on your side," I said. And they thought I was on their side.'

Emma opened her mouth to speak.

'Silence!' shouted the man, cutting off his own laughter, and raising his hand before Emma had managed to finish a word. 'I am the general of the south-eastern Unreality Institute,' he said. 'And I am not an idiot.' The general began pacing back and forth in front of the three children. He smelled of washing that had been left in the washing machine for too long. 'I would not allow you to walk out from under my nose. I would not allow you to steal the confabulation. I would not do it. No, no, I would not.'

'You're the general?' asked Oleg, very slowly realising that they were in the very worst position it was possible to be in.

'Of course I am,' said the general. 'Who else would be the general? You're certainly not the general.'

Oleg couldn't understand what had happened. How had they gone from running with the scientist to being here? Where had the scientist gone? 'You said to follow you,' he hissed at Emma.

'Because he said to follow him,' said Emma, tipping her head towards the general. 'He said he wanted to help us.'

Oleg couldn't believe it. 'And you believed him!'

'Why wouldn't I?'

'Maybe because we're trying to escape and he's the one

we're trying to escape from?'

'Silence!' screamed the general. 'Silence in the general's hall! I am the general, not you. And I say silence.'

He was ignored.

'I didn't know he was the general,' said Emma. 'He said he was on our side.'

'Remember stranger danger? Why would you believe everything everyone tells you?'

'Because it's better than believing nothing anyone tells you, because then people turn up in vans and take your friends away.'

'You're both speaking very loudly,' said Sebastian Cole.

'Shut up!' barked the general. 'Shut up, shut up, shut up!' The three children fell silent.

'Why do you want me to disappear?' asked Sebastian Cole, looking at his feet. 'I've never called you a dingo or put ham in your shoes.'

'Maybe not,' said the general. 'But you are not supposed to be here, and when you are, other things that are not supposed to be here start to pop up.' He strolled towards Sebastian and showed his teeth, which sat lopsidedly in his gums like old tombstones. 'If we don't know what's going to come next,' he said, 'then what comes next is out of our control. We must know what comes next, yes, we must. If you are here, then we don't know what comes next. If we don't know what comes next, how will we prepare for it?'

'You could just wait and see what happens,' said Oleg, surprising himself.

'And what if what happens is the end of the world?'

'It hardly ever is,' said Oleg. 'And maybe something's a bad thing at first but then it turns out to be a good thing, or it's a good thing and then a bad thing or it's another thing and then—'

'Silence!' roared the general. 'You're speaking nonsense and I've had enough, yes I have.' He dug a finger into each corner of his mouth and blew out a piercing whistle. Moments later, the room was filled with crows.

'As usual,' said the general to his crows, 'I have had to do your work for you. I have had to do it. Yes, yes, I have had to.' He coughed and spluttered. 'Take off your masks,' he boomed. 'Take them off, off, off. It doesn't matter if they see your faces now. It doesn't matter. Let them see your silly, lazy, bad-at-your-job faces.'

The crows let their masks fall.

Behind them, were faces as normal as yours or mine, only slightly more embarrassed over being disciplined in front of children. There were freckled faces, spotted faces, scarred faces, and faces that looked as though they needed a long lie-down. There were faces with toothpaste left behind on the cheeks. There were faces that had forgotten to shave.

Oleg picked out the leader with electric blue eyes whose face had hovered over his in the van. Her face was disappointingly normal. What had he been expecting? He'd been expecting them to be frightening but this one looked like someone's mum. The crow had blonde highlights and eyes rimmed with black make-up. Even her teeth were normal-sized.

'Yes,' said the general. 'I suppose you thought they were monsters of some kind. I suppose you thought they were beasts. Monsters would do their jobs far better. Beasts would be preferable. You see, each year I ask for more money in the budget, and each year I ask again, and each year they say no, no, we have other priorities, like the wars and the schools and the lampposts and …'

The general continued to talk.

Neither Oleg nor Emma listened.

Instead, Oleg leaned in to Emma and asked if she still had the snowwoman's eye.

'Yes,' she whispered. 'But how is that going to help?'

'Maybe she can still see out of it,' said Oleg. 'And maybe if you show it what's happening to us, they could come to help. It has to be night-time, they should be ready to leave the woods by now.'

'The trees,' continued the general. 'And the roads and the rivers and the traffic wardens and …'

Emma struggled to shift her hand around to where she could sink it into her pocket. When she did, she gripped the snowwoman's eye tightly, and prayed silently that it would save them.

She rolled the eye along the floor.

'And the police,' said the general. 'And the hospitals and the flowerbeds and the dustbin men and …'

Helplessly, Oleg and Emma watched the eye come to a standstill. It quivered and flopped over on one side.

'It's not working,' whispered Emma. 'Maybe it was just a stupid rock.'

'It's going to work,' said Oleg. 'It has to work.'

'And the firemen,' concluded the general. 'They use up all their budget on all those things and leave nothing for us. They think we're unimportant. We're unimportant, they think, but we're the most important subdivision of secret intelligence on this waterlogged island.' The general raised an arm into the air. 'Because we are all that stands between society and chaos!'

Which was exactly when a crack split the wall of the hall in two.

33

The army that crashed through the walls of the Institute of Unreality was unlike any army that had ever been seen before.

It was an impossible army.

It was an army that made no sense at all.

Nonetheless, it tore through the walls and launched itself at the crows.

Snowwomen rode proudly on the backs of an entire zoo of animals. Rhinos, elephants, lions, tigers, giraffes, and goats filled the hall of the green marble, each and every one of them ridden by a furious snowwoman, gesturing threateningly with their twig arms.

At their head rode the one-eyed snowwoman. She was sitting on a hairy warthog armed with fearsome tusks.

The crows were terrified. Without their masks, they were

just people, and what were people against a horde of furious snowwomen and wild animals?

'Pin them down!' ordered the one-eyed snowwoman.

The impossible army advanced.

'Stop, stop, stop,' shouted the general, cowering behind the crow with electric blue eyes. 'I am the general, and I say stop. I am the—'

He was cut off as a grizzly bear placed a paw on each of his shoulders and knocked him to the ground. The snowwoman on its back told him that if he opened his mouth again, the bear would tear off his head.

While the unmasked crows fought with the snowwomen, the scientist scurried into the hall to release the prisoners. After she'd seen them fall for the general's trick, she'd decided to wait outside and count down from one hundred. If the children had managed to get themselves out by then, she'd help them; if not, she'd have to go on alone.

'You went with the general,' said the scientist, shaking her head as she pulled apart the knots that bound Emma's hands together.

'I thought he was on our side,' explained Emma, crossly.

'But he's the general. Why would he be on your side?'

'I didn't know he was the general!' shouted Emma. 'I'm sorry I believed him, okay? I'm sorry that I'm so stupid that I believe what people say. Maybe I shouldn't. Maybe I won't next time. But yes, I did it this time, so will everybody just shut up about it until we're somewhere the ground isn't shaking and elephants aren't fighting crows and a massive black bear didn't just do a wee on my back!'

No one said anything. Emma took a deep breath.

'Sorry,' she said, shaking droplets of wee off her shirt. 'I'm done now.'

Oleg was impressed. He had never seen Emma become so un-calm. It was a good thing, he thought, to sometimes throw everything you were thinking out of your mouth in one go. It helped. It meant you didn't have so much to carry around with you. Sometimes, he thought, if you kept too much in, you'd stop wanting to get up at all; like his dad.

'Shouldn't we be escaping?' asked Oleg.

'We definitely should,' said Sebastian Cole. 'I've always wanted to escape.'

Emma bent down and picked up the eye, hurling it through the air at the snowwoman, who caught it and pushed it back into her face.

'Thank you,' Emma mouthed from across the room.

The snowwoman wiggled her twig arms, before spurring her rhino towards the closest crow.

34

With their enemies held back, it wasn't long before they were standing in the glass tunnel, the gloomy green of the forest falling over them.

The scientist led them to a section that looked like any other, crouched down, and started work on a pane of glass. She used a tiny screwdriver to draw out screws smaller than grains of rice.

The panel of glass came loose and the scientist put it to one side.

'In you go,' she said.

On all fours, they crawled through. Once they were all in, the scientist refitted the glass and wound the screws back in so that the crows wouldn't be able to see where they'd gone.

The jungle was sweltering.

It smelled of rotting wood, rushing water, and wild animals. Ancient trees were anchored by thick tangles of roots. Carpets of moss covered everything in sight. Oleg counted several species of insect and spotted a kind of golden butterfly he'd once seen in a documentary. His nervousness was quickly overtaken by curiosity, and he wished they had more time to take everything in.

Bent up against the glass ceiling was the highest tree in the forest, the one the scientist had been talking about. It was the size of a block of flats. Branches as thick as telephone poles reached towards the ground and vivid red parrots hopped between them.

Oleg screamed.

'Don't scream,' hissed the scientist. 'It's only a tree.'

'I'm not screaming at the tree,' said Oleg. 'There's a snake.' He pointed at a creature the size of a little finger wrapped around a twig.

'It's only a baby,' said the scientist.

'He doesn't like anything bigger than a cricket,' explained Emma.

They made their way along the rocky path, scrambling over heaps of roots, fallen logs, and mossy boulders.

Oleg's fright disappeared the more bugs and insects he came across. The others had to keep pestering him to hurry up. He paused for an entire minute beside a glistening blue web that stretched between two bushes. As he stood watching, a hairy spider with eyes like diamonds crept out of a hole and lumbered across its web.

'Ol,' said Emma. 'Come on.'

Reaching the tallest tree took longer than any of them had expected. There was no clear path, just spots where the undergrowth was less dense. At one point, they had to crawl through a ditch filled with mulchy leaves. After that, they helped each other over a chasm and took turns swinging over a dirty river using a loose vine.

When they reached the tree, everyone stared up at the wooden skyscraper looming over them. A4 leaves hung from its branches. It didn't look like an exit. If anything, it looked like it was in the way.

'What now?' said Emma. 'It's just a massive tree.'

'In there,' said the scientist, pointing to an arch made from one of the largest roots.

They filed in, finding a staircase that wound down into the earth. Candles lit the way. A layer of hardened wax sat on top of the uneven stairs.

As they descended the winding staircase, they heard the sound of running water. The green of the jungle faded and the air became cooler. Shadows danced across the walls.

A stronger light began to grow.

The stairs ended at a stone platform that jutted out into a

channel of water. A small wooden boat was tethered to an iron hoop. It rocked gently in the dark water. Two oars lay in the back, beside a picnic hamper and a stack of blankets.

'Here we go,' said the scientist. 'Our way out.'

'Where does it lead?' asked Oleg.

'I'm not sure. But unless it's another place like this, I suggest we all buckle in.'

One by one, they climbed in, trying to keep the boat steady.

'Bagsy not rowing,' whispered Oleg.

Each of them fitted snugly in the vessel, with their knees pressed against the back of the person in front. The scientist opened the hamper to find a thermos filled with tea, which she poured into polystyrene cups and passed around. There was no need for rowing, as the current of the water carried them along at a steady pace.

On the gently flowing stream, they cruised calmly away from the dingy compound and its masked defenders. It was not the most thrilling escape, but it was an escape, and that's what mattered.

They ate jam sandwiches and drank tea and unfolded blankets across their laps. Soon, the soft rhythm of the water had sent the children to sleep.

Some hours later, a pale crescent moon dropped into

view. Around it, the sky was packed with stars.

Emma shook Oleg awake. 'I think we're almost there,' she said. 'Wherever there is.'

Blinking awake, Oleg took in the moon. It reminded him of his scar. He realised they were free, and remembered that he wasn't going to let Dad sleep away whole days any more.

The stream carried them out of the passage and along the side of a field busy with horses, who followed the unexpected vessel as it floated past their home. Moonlight glittered off the grass as it rolled like waves in the breeze.

Finally, the boat came to a stop amongst a thicket of bulrushes.

A giant snowplough was pulled up to the riverbank.

'About time,' said the cowboy gardener, reaching down to help them up. 'I've been waiting for you.'

35

In the heart of the night, they thundered along the motorway. The scientist sat on the snowplough, behind the cowboy, with her hands on his waist. Oleg, Emma, and Sebastian Cole lay tucked in with a blanket in their trailer. They'd asked the cowboy how he'd known where they were going to be. *I just had a feeling*, was the only answer he gave them.

On this journey, no one was in danger of falling asleep.

They took turns at standing up and feeling the wind rush at their faces. Streetlights flashed past. Oncoming traffic roared.

It felt like flying, or at least they all guessed it did.

Despite the threat of crows pursuing them, it was decided that they ought to stop for food at the service station. Everyone ordered a milkshake and a burger, except for the scientist, who ordered three milkshakes and three double cheeseburgers.

'What?' she said. 'It's been a long time since I've eaten anything that didn't come out of a tin.'

Apart from an exhausted server, they were the only people there. They clustered around a circular plastic table, dabbing grease off their fingers and sucking thick milkshake up straws.

'We look like a family,' said Sebastian Cole. 'A family who has been on a long and exciting holiday packed with donkey rides and ice-creams and unexpected things falling out of the sky.'

The cowboy blushed.

The scientist laughed.

Oleg wondered whether his dad was asleep, tossing and turning in a terrible dream. Had he realised it was almost Christmas? Did he care?

'What's going to happen to the snowwomen?' Emma asked. 'Do you think the crows will capture them too?'

'It's possible,' said the scientist. 'And it's also possible that a few more impossible things will still happen. Once they're finished fighting, the snowwomen will try to get somewhere as cold as possible, somewhere they can live without melting. I'm not sure they'll reach the Arctic, but they might, with the help of their trusty steeds, make it to the peak of a snow-capped Scottish mountain.'

'I hope so,' said Emma.

'Me too,' said Oleg.

The cowboy finished off his last chip and let out a burp. 'So,' he said. 'Does anyone have any idea what comes next?' He nodded at Sebastian Cole. 'This young man seems destined to be chased wherever he goes.'

'I do,' said Emma. 'Or, maybe I do. I had an idea but I don't know if it'll work.' She blinked. 'How much longer do you think the asteroid will stay in alignment?' she asked the scientist.

Without replying, the scientist bounded outside. They followed. She was standing in the centre of the car park with her head tipped back, examining the sky. With one hand, she made a right angle and held it up against her eye. She narrowed her eyes. She doodled a calculation on her left arm. Eventually, she had their answer.

'I'd say we have a matter of hours,' she said. 'After that, the asteroid will be on its merry way through the universe. It'll be back, of course, though it's difficult to predict when.'

'How does that help?' asked Oleg. 'We can't just sit around and hope more weird stuff happens.'

'It's not that,' said Emma. 'I was thinking, if people can come out of stories, maybe they can go back into them.'

No one understood.

'Oleg's grandma is a writer,' she told them. 'What if she takes Sebastian Cole and writes him into a story? That way, they won't be able to find him, but he'll still be around. We take him out of our world and put him in one that she's made up. He can spend his days doing whatever he wants.'

They all stood in silence, thinking about it.

Could it really work?

'It's genius,' said the scientist. 'You'll be keeping him alive and there's no way they'll ever get to him. If you put him in a story, he'll be safe. Far safer than any of us.'

'Wonderful,' said Sebastian Cole. 'I've always wanted to be in a story.'

'Do you think your grandma could do it?' asked the cowboy.

'I'm not sure,' said Oleg. 'I think so. She has trouble with endings but this already has one, I guess. And if she can do it, she'll do it fast. Dad says she used to be able to get an entire book done in one night if she drank enough coffee.'

For a while, they sat deep in their own thoughts, until the cowboy humming 'Silent Night' brought them back to reality. He stopped when he noticed they were all staring at him.

'You were humming,' the scientist explained.

'Was I?' said the cowboy. 'I suppose I was. I didn't realise.'

Emma nodded. 'My mum says that every time a song comes into your head without a reason it's because someone's listening to it alone and having a cry. It is the universe's way of making sure they aren't really alone.'

'Yes,' said the scientist. 'The universe can be quite thoughtful when it wants to be.'

With that, they climbed back on to the snowplough and headed towards town.

36

They arrived outside Oleg's house just as the sun was beginning to rise from the edge of the world. The corners of the sky were turning blue and the chill of the night was drifting away, thawing the pads of snow that had built up along the streets. It was Christmas Eve and children throughout the town were dreaming of electric scooters and phones that could talk.

Oleg entered his house first, to check the coast was clear.

As usual, his dad was asleep on the sofa, wrapped in a tattered blanket.

As usual, the clicking of typewriter keys echoed overhead.

He hauled down the ladder to the attic and climbed.

'Grandma?' he called, knocking on the hatch. 'Are you there?'

'Oleg? Is that you? Where have you been?' She slid her

glasses down her nose and looked over the top of them. 'I was hungry,' she said. 'I missed my pizza.'

'Sorry, Nan, something happened. But I have friends over and we need your help. Can I bring them up?'

There was a sudden burst of rustling and shuffling. Oleg assumed she was clearing away her rubbish and hiding her half-finished stories. She'd never show anything to anyone unless it was finished, which meant no one had seen anything in years.

'Bring them up,' Grandma said.

A few seconds later everyone was standing awkwardly in the crowded attic. There wasn't a lot of room. Both adults had to crouch and Emma found herself balancing on an old trombone case. The cowboy combed a spiderweb out of his hair. The scientist shook loose a beetle from her coat.

'Isn't this nice?' said Grandma. 'I haven't had so many visitors in a long time.' She asked Oleg to translate from Polish to English for the guests, which he did. They all nodded back politely. 'Now put the kettle on,' she told him, which he did too.

While the water boiled, Grandma beckoned Sebastian Cole over.

'Fascinating,' she said, moving her face very close to his. 'It's difficult to believe he came out of nowhere.'

'Thank you,' said Sebastian Cole, in Polish. 'Sometimes I think the same thing about the entire world!'

'He speaks Polish!'

'He can do everything,' Oleg explained. 'He has a bag that makes chicken nuggets.'

'And he can make fish laugh,' said Emma.

'And he can dance.'

'And do maths.'

Sebastian Cole blushed.

Once everyone was holding a cup of tea and had found a seat amongst the piles of paper, Oleg tried to describe their situation to his grandma. She didn't seem particularly shocked by any of it. If anything, he sensed she'd been expecting something like this to happen. She nodded as he spoke.

'There are people after Sebastian,' Oleg said. 'Because this weird asteroid lines up with some other planets and impossible things happen and he's not really supposed to be here but he is. Emma thought maybe you could write him into a story; that way he'd be safe, and we could visit him if we wanted.'

Grandma thought.

And thought.

And had another cup of tea.

And thought some more.

'It will be difficult,' she said. 'I've never done it before. And it might hurt a little too.'

'I'm very good with pain,' said Sebastian Cole. 'I've been ignoring it all my life. Once, I lost a tooth and only realised when I found it at the bottom of a crisp packet.'

'Will they still come looking for him, though?' asked Oleg. 'Will they come here?'

The scientist shook her head. 'He won't show up on any of their equipment once he's moved. If he's inside a story, he won't be any danger to them. Impossible things are allowed to happen in stories; that's what they're for.'

'So it's decided?'

'I guess it is.'

'I have a question,' said Oleg.

'Go on.'

'If they're looking for made-up things that moved out of not-real life to real life, how come their equipment didn't find the cowboy?'

'It's a good question,' said the scientist. 'From what I can tell, your unusually dressed school groundskeeper has been hiding in this world for so long, and accepted as real by so many kids at the school, that this world has made him a part of itself.'

Everyone looked puzzled.

'In the beginning,' said the scientist, 'lots of people thought money was silly bits of paper, but the more people believed in it, the more real it became. When we believe in things, we give them power, and let them flourish, for better or for worse.'

Oleg nodded, satisfied with the answer.

'We'll leave you to say goodbye,' said the scientist, taking the cowboy by the hand and leading him out of the attic.

The children stood uncertainly in front of each other.

'I'll still be there,' Sebastian said, nervously. 'Won't I?' His lower lip was trembling slightly and his hands were balled in fists at his sides. It was the only time Oleg or Emma had seen him shaken. Even being imprisoned by crows hadn't made him as worried as this.

'You'll be in one of Oleg's Grandma's books,' promised Emma. 'Where no one can get to you. And she'll write it so you'll be going on adventures and trout tickling and escaping villains.'

'Could I have a treehouse?' asked Sebastian Cole.

'Of course.'

'With lots of other treehouses connected to it? And a monkey that can play chess?'

'If that's what you want.'

'What if I want it so we stay at the same school with the bald man and you don't have to go away?'

'Then Grandma will make it happen.'

'And you'll visit?'

'Always,' said Emma.

'And often,' said Oleg.

They took turns double-tapping Sebastian Cole on the forehead.

He looked confused and slightly offended. Both of them realised they'd never mentioned their way of saying goodbye. They laughed and told him what it meant.

In response, he dragged them into a three-way hug.

'This was my weekend,' he said. 'And it was truly magical.'

'It wasn't a weekend,' said Emma.

'It was to me,' said Sebastian with a grin.

Oleg hiked his T-shirt up over his face. 'We'll be downstairs if you need us,' he mumbled.

'See you on the other side,' said Emma, saluting.

Sebastian Cole crouched and scooped his hand through the air as though he were tickling an invisible fish.

Understanding what was happening, both Oleg and Emma joined in with the dance.

Not understanding what was happening, Grandma squinted through her glasses and wondered whether the three children had all been hit on the head.

Once the routine was over, they hugged again.

Sebastian dug into his bag and produced the megatron. He pressed it. Puffs of smoke rolled out from behind a stack of old boxes, which were knocked down to reveal the cardboard spaceship, looking the same as it ever had.

Oleg and Emma took one last look at their third friend. Together, they descended the ladder into the living room, where the cowboy and the scientist were watching Oleg's dad snore like a broken motor.

The cowboy patted them both on the head. 'You two best look after yourselves,' he said. 'Don't let the grass get too long and mind whoever takes over doesn't mow over Coke cans. They get all shredded and that can hurt a person.'

Confused, Emma looked to the scientist for an explanation. She shrugged.

'Wait!' the cowboy shouted, scuttling back up into the attic. Standing in front of Grandma, Sebastian, and the MicroAstral 9000, he took off his hat and pressed it to his chest. 'Is there any chance you might consider writing me into the story with the boy? This world isn't my world. I think it's time to be moving on, just so long as the next book I'm in doesn't involve everyone shooting each other.'

They stared at each other.

'I'll do what I can,' promised Grandma, who didn't need to understand the English words to know what it was the tall man dressed like a cowboy wanted from her.

'Thank you, kindly,' said the cowboy, returning his hat to his head.

And the hatch to the attic was pulled shut.

37

They slept the entire day through. At one point, Oleg's dad woke up. He saw his son, Emma, and the scientist sleeping on the floor around him, became convinced he was dreaming, and drifted back off.

Oleg dreamed of a voyage through the Arctic.

Emma dreamed of life on a steamboat headed down the Nile. She passed pyramids, lush forests, and great glass cities that climbed towards the sky.

The scientist dreamed of owning her own spaceship and using it to zip between planets populated by strangely kind and hungry aliens.

When they finally woke up, pizzas were ordered and teas were made. They watched old, half-remembered Christmas films on the TV and took it in turns to boil the kettle. The sky split open and a calm rain fell, gently speckling the windows and ticking off the roof.

There was a moment of tension when a van pulled up on to the pavement outside. They all ran to the window and pressed their faces to the glass. Through the dreary weather, it was difficult to make out much. Could the crows have come back for Sebastian?

'Is it them?' asked Emma.

'It's hard to see,' said Oleg.

The tune of 'Greensleeves' floated in over the crackle of rain.

They all fell about laughing. It was an ice-cream van, pulling up at the kerb. An ice-cream van on Christmas Eve made no sense, but Oleg and Emma decided it was just the last in a long line of impossible things. They also decided that ice-cream would be the perfect dinner and the scientist lent them enough change for four cones.

Once they were outside, they froze.

Elissa Goober was standing behind the window of the van, wearing an apron and wielding an ice-cream scoop in one hand. As soon as she saw her two classmates, her face fell. She looked like someone who wished she could be anywhere else.

'Um,' said Oleg. 'Elissa?'

'What?' said Elissa Goober, trying not to cry. 'What can I get you?'

'Are you working in an ice-cream van?'

'It's my mum's,' said Elissa.

'ELISSA!' shouted a voice from the driver's seat. 'MAKE SURE TO GIVE 'EM FLAKES. REMEMBER: NO ONE LEAVES WITHOUT A FLAKE!'

'She's not always like that,' said Elissa. 'She just gets grumpy when it's near Christmas and no one wants to buy ice-cream.'

'And she makes you work in the van?' asked Emma.

Elissa nodded, sadly. 'She says I won't get any presents otherwise.'

'But how do you revise for SATs? Or get ready for entrance exams?'

'I don't,' said Elissa. 'Mum says it doesn't matter which school I go to because I'll end up driving the van anyway. She says it's our family business. She says I'll never be an actress either, because my voice is too ugly.'

'ELISSA!' shouted her mum. 'YOU'D BETTER NOT BE CHIT-CHATTING UNLESS YOU WANT SMACK-SMACKING ROUND THE BACK OF YOUR LAZY SKULL!'

For the first time in a long time, Oleg felt very grateful for his dad, and very sorry for Elissa Goober. Sebastian must have been right about mean people being unhappy people. How, he wondered, could a parent treat their child like someone who worked for them?

'I should get back to work,' murmured Elissa. She looked up in a sudden panic. 'Please don't tell anyone at school you saw me doing this.'

'We promise,' said Emma and Oleg in unison.

Elissa lowered ice-creams out of the window to them both.

'Don't worry about paying,' she said. 'I'll tell Mum someone ran off without giving me the money.' She wiped a tear of tiredness out of her eye. 'What happened to Sebastian Cole?' she asked. 'Is he going to be okay?'

'He's going to be fine,' said Oleg. 'I'll give you his address and you can write to him.'

Elissa Goober smiled.

'Happy Christmas, Elissa,' said Emma.

'Happy Christmas, idiots,' said Elissa.

✳

At midnight, Grandma came downstairs. Her eyes were red and her hands were shaky.

It was the first time in years she'd left the attic. Smiling, she felt the soft carpet under her feet.

'It's done,' she said, setting a stack of paper down on the kitchen counter. 'I'll call my old publisher tomorrow.'

'You really wrote a whole book?' asked Oleg. 'Just now? With Sebastian and the cowboy in it?'

'I did,' said Grandma. 'And I have you both to thank for it. Thank you for trusting me with your story.'

'Thank you for saving Sebastian Cole.'

'I'm going to have a lie-down,' said Grandma. 'I've had far too much coffee and my wrists feel like they're about to fall off.'

'Grandma?' said Oleg.

'Yes?'

'You've left the attic.'

'So I have,' said Grandma with surprise. 'I should probably make a habit of doing so more often.'

'It's Christmas, by the way.'

'Is it really?'

She shuffled around the kitchen, walked a slow lap of the garden, then came back inside and fell asleep in the armchair. Oleg dabbed the rain off her face then draped a blanket over her lap. He watched his grandma and his dad sleeping and he wondered if things would change or if they would go on as they always had. Now Sebastian was gone, would there still be space left for unexpected things?

★

That night, Oleg slept over at Emma's, while the scientist said goodbye but promised to return. They spent most of the evening playing Snap in the summer house. Everything felt too quiet without Sebastian Cole. There was no one to act inappropriately excited or come out with strange things that made no sense. And nothing impossible happened either. The rain fell steadily, the sky darkened.

Oleg grumbled. 'We'll have to start revising again soon,' he said. 'And you'll have to take the test for St Mary's.'

'Mum will make me,' said Emma. 'But I had an idea. If I just put "sponge" as the answer to every question then I'll never get in and we'll both go to St Jude's.'

Oleg laughed then shook his head. 'If you get in,' he said, 'you have to go. It's supposed to be way better. They have electric boards and virtual reality headsets and teachers that want to be teachers.'

'But I won't know anyone.'

'We'll know each other and we can just text in lessons then meet after school. The people can't be worse than Scott or Callie or Tom Runkle. As long as we're not mean, I don't think people will start rumours that we have fifteen toes.'

Emma thought about it and dropped her head on to Oleg's shoulder. 'Why aren't you scared? I thought you were scared.'

'I am,' said Oleg. 'But I think that weird general was wrong.

Just because you don't know what's going to happen, doesn't mean the world will end.' Oleg swallowed. 'Anyway,' he said, 'we'll have Grandma's book so we won't forget anything.'

Emma's mum appeared outside. She was holding four bulging carrier bags and grinning like a clown.

'I've got cake!' she said.

'Don't you have work?' asked Emma, sitting up and beaming. 'You said you'd be working.'

Mum shook her head. 'I quit,' she said. 'Someone complained that the coffee tasted like soil-soup, so I tore off my apron, told them to make it themselves, and left. I'm not working over Christmas.'

Oleg and Emma both laughed. 'But can you afford to quit? I thought we needed the money.'

Mum held up an envelope. 'This came in the post,' she said. 'It's a cheque and it's more than enough to pay off the debt. I've already called college and they said I could go back next term. I'm going to finish my course.'

'But who sent it?'

'I'm not entirely sure, but it's made out to my name. I think it came from Japan. Anyway, you're not supposed to look a gift horse in the mouth.'

'What's a gift horse?' asked Emma.

Mum thought. 'I'm not entirely sure,' she said. 'But I do

know it's a good thing. Now I can spend more time with you. And we can get a TV again.'

'I don't want a TV,' said Emma.

'No,' said her mum. 'Neither do I.'

They spent the night playing board games and eating sweet things with Pip, Oliver, and Emma's mum. Seeing Emma with her mum made Oleg feel grateful and happy but a little lost too.

Oliver cooked a turkey that melted like butter in their mouths.

Pip handed out bright papier-mâché presents.

Emma forced Oleg to perform the trout-tickling dance.

And her mum made tea for a team of blue-lipped carol singers who were soaked through with unexpected rain.

Later, they all fell asleep in front of the space where the TV used to be, their mouths dark with chocolate as the last hours of Christmas ticked by.

The next morning, Oleg raced through the door of his house and ripped the blanket off his sleeping dad.

'You have to get up!' he shouted. 'Get up, get up, get up!'

Blearily, Dad opened his eyes. He had no idea what was going on. Oleg kept shouting.

'I know it seems terrible now but sometimes random impossible things happen! You can't give up on the world. It's the only world you get.'

Dad blinked the sleep out of his eyes. 'All right,' he said.

'Not all right,' said Oleg. 'Get up right now. You missed Christmas.'

Oleg whipped him with the blanket.

'That hurt,' said Dad.

'Good,' said Oleg.

'Put the kettle on,' said Dad.

'I already did,' said Oleg.

Once they both had strong, sweet cups of tea between their hands, they sat facing each other on the sofas.

'I've been away for three days and you didn't notice a thing,' said Oleg.

'You have? Where have you been?'

'It doesn't matter. All that matters is if you forget people, they disappear. You put them in a room and no one remembers them and they fade away and it's like they never existed.'

'Oleg, mate, calm down.'

'I am calm.'

Oleg took deep breaths and sipped his tea. His dad ran a hand through his messy nest of hair. He sat like a person who'd found themselves in a body that was far too large for them to know what to do with. He wasn't quite sure where to put his spindly legs or dinner-plate hands, so he moved them constantly as though he was nervous.

'You know what I did while you were out?' his dad said.

'What?' asked Oleg, convinced the answer was going to be 'sleep'.

'I started reading your nan's new book,' said Dad. 'She finished an entire new one, it was lying on the side. And do you know what? It's incredible. It's funny and it's sad and it's got this weird kid called Sebastian Cole in it.'

Despite himself, Oleg chuckled.

'I'm sorry, okay? I didn't realise how much it was affecting you. I've been selfish, I can see that. I've been letting everything get on top of me, without thinking about how it must make you feel. It's just, I feel useless. I feel useless so I'm being useless, rather than trying to change things.'

'That's okay,' said Oleg, who suddenly didn't want to make his dad more upset than he already was. He saw for the first time how much his dad's face had changed. There were silver sparks in his overgrown beard and mazes of wrinkles under his eyes.

'No,' said his dad. 'It's not okay. But it will be. You'll see. If your nan can get back on track, so can I.'

'Good.'

'And I'm sorry I didn't get you anything for Christmas.'

'That's okay, I didn't want anything anyway.'

They hugged.

Oleg held on tight to the reassuring lump that was his father.

And the next morning, a letter came in the post. It was a letter from the head of a large company who dealt with kitchen supplies. They were, the letter claimed, Europe's leading supplier of cheese graters.

Dear Mr Duchownik,

It has recently come to my attention, thanks to a rather rambunctious young man in a long scarf, that you are currently unemployed. After reviewing your sales record, I find this impossible to comprehend, and I would like to offer you a job as our south-west sales representative. I eagerly await your response. If you could start on Monday, Mr Duchownik, that would be wonderful.

Yours,

Elliot Iole

Snakebread Kitchens, Tokyo and Beyond

38

Things changed at school. After spending two days locked in a cupboard together, Mr Clay and Mr Morecombe found a way of overcoming their differences. Mr Morecombe said it was silly to still be angry about something someone had done as a child. Mr Clay said he couldn't understand why he'd been so cruel. The way he'd treated Mr Morecombe had followed him through his adult years like a raincloud.

'I'm sorry,' he said, for the hundred and eleventh time.

'It doesn't matter,' said Mr Morecombe. 'Let's just make the most of now.'

They found a Dungeons and Dragons board at the back of the lost property cupboard and organised a game involving all the members of staff. As their pieces gallivanted around the board, dragons were slayed and entire villages were rescued.

A few days later, once everyone had been freed, a new member of staff joined the school. It was the scientist, who it turned out had a name. Miss Chang taught physics and biology. She took the children on expeditions through nearby woodland and showed them documentaries about life at the bottom of the ocean.

Once a year, she had parents fill in permission slips for the children to spend a whole night sleeping at school. They'd all take sleeping bags up to the roof and watch the stars.

'There's Orion,' she'd say.

And:

'That's Cassiopeia, the queen who thought of nothing but her own beauty.'

Both Oleg and Emma became friendlier with Elissa Goober. They never became friends, exactly – all of the impossible things had already happened – but still, they managed to get along most days.

And not long after they saw her dishing out ice-cream, Elissa's mum's ice-cream van was confiscated: a health inspector had found copious amounts of goat poo in the freezer. Elissa was now free to revise. She did very well in her SATs and left home as soon as she was old enough, to start a career in the courtroom.

The snowwomen didn't make it to the Arctic, only to a

patch of land near a new housing estate, where they became a lake. To wake up to an unexpected lake was the best late Christmas present the children on that estate had ever had. After that, it froze every winter without fail, and they spent their holidays ice-skating and their summers cannonballing through the cool water.

Oleg and Emma grew up the way that most children tend to do: slowly at first, then all at once. They went to different secondary schools and met new friends, but never left each other behind. More than once, the new groundskeeper at their old school found himself chasing two increasingly tall teenagers out of a den at the edge of the field.

Emma is a journalist now, travelling the globe in search of stories showing the strangest, saddest, and most inspiring things people are capable of. Every time her mum sees one of her daughter's stories in the newspaper, she cuts it out and glues it into a book bigger than the biggest bible.

Oleg is an entomologist, not to be confused with an etymologist or an endomologist. He treks through jungles, forests, and woods in search of new species of insect. So far, he's found one. He named it Sebasteus Colea.

Oleg's dad worked his way up the kitchen supply business. He manages a team of four now. Every summer, he goes to the Amalfi Coast and sleeps under the sun for a week to recharge his batteries.

Emma's mum earned her business degree and opened a restaurant with her son, Oliver, as the chef. The restaurant is inside a huge treehouse that encompasses four trees in the Wickerly Wood. If you ever go, I'd recommend the pumpkin lasagne.

Sometimes Oleg's dad takes Oleg's grandma to eat there. They always order at least six courses, and sit for hours and hours, telling each other stories and jokes, and watching the sun set behind the trees. When it's time to close, Emma's mum joins them for a glass of wine.

They both miss their children, whose jobs mean they're out of the country more than they're in it.

But every year, near Christmas, no matter where they are in the world, Oleg and Emma speak to each other on the phone for an entire night. Over that night, they read the book written by Oleg's grandmother and remember their time with Sebastian Cole. The book, by the way, is called *The Impossible Boy*.

Tap.

Tap.

NOTES

✳ The green children of Woolpit did exist and did appear in Suffolk in the twelfth century. No one knows who they were or where they came from. They spoke in a strange language and ate only raw beans.

✳ Asteroid B 612 is home to the Little Prince, as told in the story by Antoine de Saint-Exupery.

✳ Baron Franz Xaver Von Zach created the 'celestial police' at the end of the eighteenth century. They were a team of astronomers tasked with searching out a planet that had gone missing.

✳ The Institute of Unreality does not, officially, exist.

ACKNOWLEDGEMENTS

Thanks to Dan, co-creator of Sebastian Cole on bored schooldays. Thanks to Renata, who was woken up when I had the idea for this book. Thanks to Jan and Katy, the two sanest and kindest people either side of the Danube. Thanks to Matthew for handling the adult parts. Thanks to Tig for being patient and kicking the story into a better shape. Thanks to Sarah, Ruth, and everyone else at Hachette for their hard work, energy, and flattery. Thanks to you too, especially if you read this far, because it's not really part of the story and it was probably quite boring.

LOOK OUT

FOR A BRAND NEW ADVENTURE FROM BEN BROOKS

THE GREATEST INVENTOR

COMING OCTOBER 2020!